praise for

THAT'S

"I love this book! J... Texas cowgirl had m... time in the country. ... our relationships ar... lenging things get running a three-hundred-acre ranch, Jules is strengthened by her deep bonds with her quirky family, their countless ranch animals, and the neighbors who never hesitate to come to their rescue. Perhaps most remarkable is the fact that this incredibly well-crafted novel was written by a seventeen-year-old!"

—JULIE MIRLICOURTOIS, former producer for
Oprah Winfrey, Award-winning TV producer

"Juliette Turner has given us an everyday heroine who takes on life with a steadfast faith, a delightful unconquerable spirit, and the unconditional love of her mom. A fun and poignant tale that will inspire and entertain—a must read!"

—CHIP FLAHERTY, cofounder Walden Media

"A combination of *Little House on the Prairie* and *Lassie*, seventeen-year-old Juliette Turner's first novel is based on her real-life experiences in New York City and on her Texas ranch with actress/political activist mom, Janine Turner. Juliette's fresh voice and honest approach are engaging from page one. Hope there are more sequels to come!"

—JOCELYN WHITE, award-winning TV and radio
journalist, creator/host of the syndicated TV
shows *Pawsitive Entertainment* and *Designing Texas*.

"I love being able to share Juliette's book with my daughter, who loves reading more than anything else in the world! Juliette's flair for writing really brought this story alive for both of us. Her story has been inspirational to my daughter, who will soon have her own teenage obstacles to overcome, and to me, who will soon be dealing with those teenage years! We look forward to reading *That's Not Hay in My Hair* again!"

—KELLIE RASBERRY, cohost of the *Kidd Kraddick Morning Show* and cohost of *Dish Nation*

"*That's Not Hay in My Hair* is replete with side-splitting laughs, heart-wrenching tears, and surprising life lessons learned down on the farm."

—MIDWEST BOOK REVIEW

"A boisterous Texas howdy should be the reader's greeting for Juliette Turner's *That's Not Hay in My Hair*. Ms. Turner enlivens a sixth grader, Jules, and her Texas family with a rollicking extravaganza of life at the Mockingbird Hill ranch. A love of animals—especially horses, longhorns, and dogs—reveals to the reader some strong story development throughout the novel. Ms. Turner's affectionate portrayals of Mom, Mimi, and Grandpa give a warmhearted vision of family life. Congratulations are sent to Ms. Turner for this Texas treat."

—JAMES INGRAM, former fifth grade teacher at Eagle Mountain Elementary

"Miss Juliette Turner has done it again! Her newest book is another literary triumph for this extraordinary young author, reminding us once again that her talent and wisdom trump her age! *That's Not Hay in My Hair* is a heartwarming tale that leads the reader on a journey to find the true meaning of home and happiness. This is a delightful read, for both those who are young enough to begin their own journey and those of us old enough to have already traveled the road."

—NANCY K. ARNOLD, retired teacher and children's author of *Patriotic Pups* and *Pioneer Pups*

THAT'S NOT HaY
iN MY HaiR

Other Books by Juliette Turner

Our Constitution Rocks!

Our Presidents Rock!

THAT'S NOT HAY IN MY HAIR

Juliette Turner

ZONDER**kidz**

ZONDERKIDZ

That's Not Hay in My Hair
Copyright © 2016 by Juliette Turner

This title is also available as a Zondervan ebook.
Visit www.zondervan.com/ebooks.

Requests for information should be addressed to:
Zonderkidz, *3900 Sparks Dr. SE, Grand Rapids, Michigan 49546*

ISBN 978-0-310-73244-0

Cover design: Brand Navigation
Cover photo: Getty, iStock, Shutterstock
Interior design: Denise Froehlich

Printed in the United States of America

16 17 18 19 20 21 22 23 24 /DCI/ 20 19 18 17 16 15 14 13 12 11 10 9 8 7 6 5 4 3 2

To my family, friends, and pets who brought this book to life.

one

Beep, beep, beep. My alarm clock buzzed furiously from my bedside table, trying to awaken me. I rolled over and slammed my hand on the snooze button, silence once again entering my room. The clock read 7:15. I had almost fallen asleep again when a loud car horn startled me into a sitting position in my bed. Stumbling over to my window, I peered down to see what all the commotion was about. Yellow taxicabs driven by angry, impatient drivers dotted Madison Avenue, and the air was filled with a cacophony of blaring car horns, shouting pedestrians, and the muffled coos of street pigeons. There appeared to be an argument between two taxi drivers in the middle of the intersection. I shrugged and turned away. *Typical New York City*, I thought.

I looked at the wall behind my desk, hoping to locate my Peanuts calendar. As always, it was hidden somewhere behind Polaroid photos of my friends and me, Playbill covers from musicals I had seen, and posters I had purchased from New York museums. My eyes grazed over the giant collage of van Gogh's landscapes, Renoir's elegant portraits of little girls in red-sashed dresses, Degas's ballerinas, and pictures of the Guggenheim Museum, Central Park, and the Empire State Building, along with Playbills from *My Fair Lady*, *Sunday in the Park with George*, and *The Lion King*, until I finally found Snoopy's face—my calendar. *Ah, finally. Now, today is Monday, June fifteenth* . . . The calendar reminded me that it was the first Monday of my summer vacation. My mood immediately brightened.

A little sticky note reading "End-of-Year Party" hung precariously in Monday's box on the calendar, informing me that, although I was free from the monotony of school, I still had one more commitment to fulfill. Another sticky note hung in the box for Wednesday, June 24. It read "Move Day." I smiled and looked at the cowboy hat dangling from my desk chair. *Texas, here I come.*

After tripping over the moving boxes scattered all over the floor, I squeezed into my small bathroom—and by small, I mean very small. The bathtub took up three-quarters of the floor; the toilet, which protruded from the wall right beside the bathtub, filled up half of the remaining space; and the sink jutted into the doorway, making it a feat simply to enter the room. The walls resembled the ancient Roman baths: long cracks lined the yellowing tile and the once-white grout was now a dark gray. Rust adorned the faucet handle and the thick, black New York soot traced the corners of the age-distorted mirror. *Glamorous New York.* Disregarding the grit and grime to which I was now immune, I curled into my pink puffy robe, stepped into my pink, bunny-shaped house shoes, and quickly washed my face. After finding my face and teeth clean enough for my liking, I threw my hair into a ponytail and walked into the narrow hallway.

"Howdy! When did you wake up?" New York had not affected Mom's southern belle accent in the slightest. *At least she sounds rested.*

"Good morning, Mom," I replied, clasping my favorite pink flower hair clip to the top of my ponytail. The kitchen smelled amazing. I was so entranced by the aroma of breakfast cooking and the roar of my empty stomach that I almost tripped over our one-hundred-pound, aptly named yellow lab, Chubbs. Chubbs completely blocked the entrance to the kitchen, begging for some of the heavenly-smelling food that had my mouth watering as well.

The kitchen was truly no larger than my bathroom. No joke. Imagine an airplane lavatory. Add in a stove, dishwasher, sink, refrigerator, and water dispenser, and you have the size of our New York City–style kitchen. Needless to say that in the already-cramped quarters, there was very little room for two people, let alone a large dog.

"What could you possibly be cooking that could smell so good?" I asked, my nose in the air, trying to sniff in as much of the wafting aroma as was humanly possible.

"Oh, I'm just fixing eggs and bacon."

Bacon. When is the last time I had that delicious breakfast delight? Mom could never eat food products containing MSG or nitrates, so bacon was a rarity in our household—not to mention my diet as a whole was considerably bland and "all natural."

"Today must be special, then?" I asked Mom with a little confusion.

"Well, you have your end-of-school party today, and I thought you deserved a treat for finishing your fifth-grade year with straight As!" Mom cheered, getting so excited that she flipped the bacon with a little too much fervor and sent a small slice flying onto Chubbs's paws. That little slice was gone and in Chubbs's stomach before I could blink. Mom shoveled the bacon and some eggs onto my plate and some eggs onto hers. "You hungry?"

Chubbs quickly scrambled backward like a Mack truck to allow Mom to exit the kitchen. The hallways in our humble New York City abode were far too narrow for us to simply walk around our slightly obese dog, and poor Chubbs was simply unable to turn around in the tight quarters.

Since our apartment had only four rooms, our kitchen table was in the living room / piano room / dining room. The table, therefore, displayed quite a collection of items: Mom's antique candelabras, towering stacks of books from the multitude of museums we had visited, picture frames displaying our family, stacks of old manuscripts from Mom's most recent book, and the feeding station for Sparkle—our black-and-white cougar-sized cat. Not to mention the recent addition of the still-empty moving boxes, which leaned against the table. Such cramped living quarters were the status quo for the New York lifestyle: money buys a lot less in the Big Apple than it does anywhere else. The spacious penthouse apartments overlooking Central Park were for those who enjoyed large monthly paychecks. Many of my schoolmates resided in such glorious apartments, so whenever my friends came over to visit, their parents' faces resembled Janet Leigh's in *Psycho* upon seeing the "horror" of our tiny space. But I didn't care; the apartment suited me just fine.

"How was your sleep?" I asked Mom while reveling in bacon-induced euphoria.

"Fine, thank you, and chew with your mouth closed," Mom reprimanded. I shut my mouth. "How was *your* sleep?" she added, readjusting her gold-rimmed glasses.

"Oh, good. Just not long enough, as usual," I replied, trying to brush Sparkle's tail out of my face. He had nearly disrupted my entire plate by skidding onto the table to join us for our morning meal. Slowly inching his paw closer to my plate, he eyed my last slice of bacon, hoping I wouldn't see if he swatted off a piece.

As I munched away, Mom shared what she had just read in the *New York Times* and what she had heard on Fox News Channel the night before. "They say the election is going to be brutal this cycle." Mom sighed. I grunted into my orange juice glass. It seemed to me that everything in politics was brutal these days—an opinion my grandmother voiced every time I mentioned my political aspirations. "It's an important election too. Oh God, be with our county!" Mom wailed, scooting back her chair.

After breakfast, I helped Mom clean the kitchen, squeezing around her every time I wanted to reach the sink. When Mom finally motioned for me to start getting ready for the party, I eagerly left the stuffy kitchen and entered my bathroom once more. I hopped into the shower/bathtub to wash my hair, successfully flooding the bathroom in the process since the shower curtain failed to constrain the spray of the lime-covered showerhead. The builder of the apartment had the wonderful idea of placing the showerhead in such a position that it projected water across the bathtub and onto the floor instead of down the grimy old drain. After filling my bathroom with enough water to buoy Noah's ark, I used all of my towels to dry the floor instead of myself. *Hand towels work to dry my hair, right?*

Then came the biggest feat I had yet to face: makeup. Mom had given me permission to wear it, as it was, after all, a special occasion. In my mind, I could see exactly what to do and what brushes to apply where; in reality, however, my inexperienced hand sent mascara all over my face and light pink lipstick way too far off my lips. My reflection in the mirror quickly transformed from an eleven-year-old girl to the Joker from the Batman movie *The Dark Knight*. I washed my face and decided to attend the party au naturel. My grandmother would have been appalled.

Next came the big decision of what to wear. I opened my closet door, sending a cascade of gym shorts, socks, and uniform skirts onto my feet. My closet was originally the size of, let's say, an upright coffin, but once I added in all of my puffy dresses, plastic drawers from the Container Store overflowing with hair accessories, and the dirty socks I meant to wash a month ago, there really was no way to close the door without applying a large amount of pressure.

"What to wear, what to wear," I asked myself, looking forlornly into the confusing jumble of my closet. What's more, a magical little fairy had apparently peeked into my closet in the middle of the night and said *"poof,"* shrinking my clothes two sizes. This was the problem with wearing a uniform to school: it made the school week very simple, but when the time came to wear real clothing, nothing fit. Sorting through my clothes, I flung all the "absolutely not" dresses onto my bed until I finally found my favorite pink-and-white-checkered sundress. "Hey, Mom, what do you think about this dress?" I asked.

Mom walked in with Sparkle the cougar-cat thrown over her shoulder like a shawl. "Oh no, that looks like a picnic blanket," she said. I was aghast. *Is my fashion sense so horrible that I gravitate toward picnic blankets?*

"Wear that dress. It looks so cute on you." She pointed to a burgundy, long-sleeved, puffy-skirted, itchy, tight, absolutely-not-my-type dress that lay on the top of my bed. Sparkle turned his head to see and immediately began purring in agreement.

"*Cute?* Baby ducks are cute," I exclaimed.

"And everybody loves baby ducks!" Mom said, smiling. As she walked out of my room, Sparkle's ears bobbed up and down from over Mom's shoulder. I grumbled, resigned to the fact that I must now wear my least favorite dress.

Now it was time to address the stockings saga. I plopped down on the dog-and-cat-hair-covered floor Mom had vacuumed just yesterday and dug through my stocking drawer, finding them all to be either too snug, snagged, or pink with green stripes—don't ask why I had that last pair.

"Mom? Do you have any stockings I could borrow?"

"Yes. Just go look in my drawer!" she said from her bathroom. I wandered into Mom's bedroom and stared at her antique chest of drawers, trying to decipher how to open the drawers without pulling off the handles in the process. Finally, after what felt like years of searching, I found a pair that would work. On the way back to my room, I glanced at the kitchen clock and couldn't believe my eyes.

"Mom, it's ten forty-five!" I yelled. I heard a crash from the bathroom. "We're supposed to leave by eleven!"

"Holy Moses!" I heard Mom exclaim. Something fell in the bathroom. "Ouch!" This exclamation was followed by another crash.

I rushed back to check on her. "Are you okay?" I asked, trying not to giggle, for it was a very comedic sight.

"Yeah, I . . . just . . . hit . . . my . . . toes . . . on . . . the . . . sink," Mom said, holding her foot and hopping around the hallway while barely avoiding Chubbs, who was trying to back up again.

"Do you need some ice?"

"No," Mom drawled, practicing her deep-breathing exercises. With that I left the scene, running to change into my dress. I really had to hurry if I wanted to get to the party on time. If I wasn't on time, Mrs. Omega—the strict, overbearing, snobby, tyrannical schoolmarm—would give me a detention, even though school was officially over. As I skidded into my bedroom, I found my burgundy dress on the floor. Creampuff, my high-maintenance white minia-ture poodle, was tearing at it with all her might.

"Creampuff!" I growled, snatching my dress from the dog's paws. Upon whisking the dress off the floor, I revealed Creampuff's favorite bunny toy. Anytime she was without that toy for more than five seconds, she went into separation anxiety mode. Now she dived on top of it and began licking it like the most content dog in the world.

Examining my dress for damage, I found a little clawed tear in the chiffon that my grandmother would have called "the end of the world." I prayed no one would notice it and threw the dress over my body. While attempting to zip up the endless zipper on my back, I began searching for my shoes.

Oy vey, I thought to myself, finding only one of my brand-new patent-leather boots in my closet. *I try so hard to stay organized.* I shuffled around the apartment, tugging at the zipper while looking for the other boot.

"No!" I gasped, finding it on Chubbs's red dog bed under the piano. "How could this get any worse?" As I picked up my shoe—or, more accurately, what was left of my shoe—I lamented my darling dog's horrible shoe-eating obsession. She had eaten almost one entire boot, including the sequin flowers and the zipper, leaving only the sole. I sadly picked up my shoe's remains and buried them beside its mate in my closet's Dirty Sock Burial Ground. *I definitely do not look forward to packing that into a box.*

"Now what shoes do I wear?" I asked my reflection in the mirror. I looked at Chubbs, who was sleeping soundly on my pink floral carpet. Sighing heavily, I dug through my closet in an attempt to find my shoe pile. After searching for some time, I began, out of desperation, throwing every solid object my hand touched onto my bedroom floor, just hoping for a matching pair of shoes. I bumped my hand blindly into some miscellaneous object. I pulled, tugged, huffed, and puffed, and finally the thing let loose. However, it wasn't my shoe. It was my Starbucks coffee cake from four months ago, which had obviously fallen out of my pink coat's pocket.

"Yuck!" I yelled. Chubbs sat up with a start. *"Food?"* her face asked.

Mom announced her arrival behind me by running into my doorframe. "Holy Moses! Are you almost ready?" Mom asked, grimacing as she now held her knee. Upon seeing the moldy lump in the middle of my room, she asked, "What in the world is that?"

"Uh . . ." I hesitated. "Just an old coffee cake from Starbucks."

"Why was that in your closet?" Mom gasped.

"It fell out of my coat pocket. I was trying to find my shoes."

"Where are your shoes?"

"Well, the patent-leather ones are probably digesting in Chubbs's stomach right now, so I am trying to find my sandals."

At that exact moment, I looked over my shoulder to find Chubbs beginning to throw up . . . parts of my boot.

"Chubbs, no!" I shouted. Alas, it was too late.

"What is the matter now— Oh, *poor* Chubbs!" Mom cooed after the shoe was successfully regurgitated.

"What about 'Oh, poor Jules's shoe'?" I asked in distress.

I begrudgingly walked over to Chubbs to see if she was feeling okay. As I knelt down I saw that she had thrown up all the little sequins into a slimy version of their former flower shape. At that moment I wondered if I had seen too much modern art.

After searching a bit more, I found my other good shoes hiding under a pile of purses and scarves. I thanked heaven above that my grandmother had given me these sandals when she visited from Texas. Without them, I would have had to wear my flip-flops to the party. Then Mrs. Omega really would have been mad. She once sent a girl home from school when her knee socks weren't the "right height" and even chased a girl's father down the hallway after he tried to tie his daughter's shoe. She was so irrational, even parents feared her presence.

"I'm ready!" I called, skidding into the hallway. Mom was still trying to decide what to wear. Her blow-dried hair looked like Julia Roberts's hair in *Steel Magnolias*.

"Okay. Make sure we have our purses, and then I'll be ready," Mom replied. I gathered Mom's purse from the kitchen table, swung my small satchel onto my shoulder, and collapsed into a chair by the front door. Sparkle sat on the shelves beside me, swinging his tail back and forth, casually wondering why I was so out of breath. As I waited, I looked up at the portrait that hung on the wall, a portrait of Mom's beloved palomino mare, Maggie. I had seen that painting my entire life, and had always been amazed by the beauty and soul of the animal. Supposedly, I had met Maggie when I was much younger, but I couldn't remember much about her at all.

Mom came around the corner at 11:05 in black slacks and a white linen business jacket, knocking me out of my daze. "You ready?" I asked her. She stepped into her high-heeled platform shoes, brushed her bangs out of her eyes, and nodded. I swung open the off-white, battered door and we exited into the hallway together. Mom locked the door as I rang the elevator bell. A loud *buzz* resonated through the fluorescent-lit hallway. Then everything was quiet again. No sound came from the other two apartments on the third floor, and the only audible noises were the footsteps of the little baby on the floor above us and the sonorous ticking of Mom's watch. *Tick, tock, tick, tock* . . . Anxiously, I tapped my toe.

"I guess Max is sleeping—again." Max, short for Maximillian, was one of the five doormen/elevator operators who all happened to be Polish. Dear old Max, who could barely speak English, was known to frequently fall asleep.

We decided to take the stairs instead. I sprinted down two stairs at a time and reached the ground level before Mom, who was struggling to keep her shoes from flying off her feet. I peeked in Max's office and saw that he was, in fact, asleep, his feet propped up on his old desk and his chin resting on his rotund chest. I was about to pass by quietly, not wanting to disturb him (for he was also known for his endless chatter), when an antiquated phone started ringing loudly from the wall. Max's large dark eyes flew open and he leaped up with a start, disturbing a large stack of papers on the cluttered desk, which subsequently crashed to the ground. Before Max could gather himself, the phone had stopped ringing. "Hi," I whispered.

"Oh, 'ello! How are you doday?" Max asked, stumbling out of his office.

"We are great! How are you?" Mom asked as she walked by. I snuck a glance at the mirrored wall on the opposite side of the hallway and resituated the clip that was sliding down my hair.

"Wonderful, have a gud day!" Max called in his thick accent, waving after us. We waved back before pushing through the doors and onto the busy New York street.

Then came the Battle of the Cabs. I held out my hand, just trying to get a cabbie's attention. Three zoomed by, barreling around corners and dashing through the inter-section. This was one thing I would not miss about New York: the heavy reliance on unpredictable transportation. Mom had assured me that people in Texas used their own cars to go places. No more Battle of the Cabs for me.

Finally, a cab screeched to a halt in front of us. "Phew!" Mom sighed, collapsing onto the cracked taxi seat. I climbed in after her. "Put on your seatbelt," Mom mut-tered before I even had a chance to sit down. I smirked. People in the city usually don't use seatbelts in taxis; in fact, Mom had informed me that seatbelts in cabs were a rather recent addition. Yet Mom, being her usual self, decided that "safety always comes first" and required I buckle up *every* time I was in a moving vehicle.

"The Metropolitan Museum, please, on 82nd and 5th Avenue," Mom told the taxi driver. The cab dashed off a little too fast for our taste, making a sharp turn off of Madison Avenue, the wheels squealing.

The Met was one of the school's favorite field trip locations, for the school prided itself on being "one thousand steps from the Metropolitan Museum of Art," and so it was naturally the location of the end-of-year party. I cannot count how many fire drills I had endured, staring at Central Park and the Met, wishing I was walking through the American Wing or the recent Egyptian exhibit instead of standing idly on the sidewalk.

"Where are you two from?" the cabdriver asked in his distinct accent. I turned my head away from the window and toward the location of the voice.

"Texas, originally," Mom said, trying to be nice.

"Ah, Texas! You know George Bush?"

"Yes, we do," Mom said.

"Oh . . . Tell him hi," he said.

"Okay, we will." Mom looked slyly at me out of the corner of her eye as she attempted to cover a laugh. I looked down at the small taxi television and watched NY1 reporting on the weather forecast for the week.

"How do you like the city?" the driver asked.

"It's busy and crowded," Mom said.

"I like it!" I replied. I rather enjoyed the city, the hustle and bustle of it all.

"It is different than Texas?" the driver asked.

"Very different," Mom answered. "Can't wait to be back." She pulled out her phone and looked at a text message someone had sent her. I peered through the clouded plastic that separated the driver's area from the backseat to find out where we were. My view of the street, however, was obstructed by a large dream catcher dangling from the rearview mirror. Additionally, I saw the driver staring at me through the rearview mirror, which concerned me since he was not watching the road. To my relief, he soon focused his eyes forward again.

A much-wanted silence filled the car. For a second.

"So what do you want to talk about?" the cabdriver asked.

Hoping he would catch the hint if I didn't respond, I looked down at the small television to watch a cook in a small pizzeria swirl dough around his hand until it was the size of a small table. *Who would ever eat a pizza that big?*

The brakes screeched under the car, the sudden stop slamming me against the tattered seatbelt. We had come to a halt in front of the large Roman-style building I knew to be the Met. Mom pulled out her credit card to pay.

"You can't use credit card. Not working," the cabdriver said.

"It was just working," I said. I had just seen the credit card option appear on the small screen when the cab stopped. It had turned mysteriously black right before I had a chance to hit "credit" on the screen.

"He wants us to pay him cash," Mom whispered, rummaging through her purse. "I didn't bring enough cash," she told the driver after a brief pause. "Sir, if you want your money, let me use my card."

"*Only cash!* You can't use card!" The cabdriver was obviously getting upset.

"We don't have any cash with us!" I piped in. Mom gave me the "You are too young to use that tone" glare.

"Fine! Use the card!" the cabdriver yelled, slamming his hands onto the wheel. "Crazy Texans," he said under his breath. Mom swiped her card through the machine and we slipped out of the cab. Mom threw a flyer for her newly released book onto the seat behind her. She always did that—for marketing, she said.

"Have a good day," I said as I closed the door. He sped off almost before the door latched. "Well, that was joyous."

The sidewalk surged with an ocean of people that parted around us as we made our way to the steps. A large group of excited college-aged girls huddled into a picture, pointing at the Met behind them. Several people perused the street vendors dotting the sidewalk, selling paintings of Times Square, hats, etchings of Central Park, or designer purses sold at an insanely cheap price.

As I looked up at the mammoth building, I smiled. I loved this museum and the art that spanned so many centuries. While I walked up the many stairs, a large poster hanging from the entablature caught my eye. The poster displayed a magnificent, rich painting of a man trying to control two huge stallions that had reared into the air, fire blazing behind their eyes. The man wore a flowing red cape and stood on rocky ground. The background was black, accentuating the colors of the horses. There was something majestic about that painting . . . about those horses . . .

A flock of city pigeons flew off the top of the stairs, shocking me out of my daze. I ducked and Mom laughed. "How are you going to take Texas if you're scared by a flock of pigeons?"

I giggled and we entered the museum through the revolving doors. A faint hum resounded off the museum walls, coming from the many people who milled around the large atrium. Lines of people gathered around a circular information desk in the center of the large room, a mainstay in an otherwise chaotic scene.

"Ready?" Mom asked me, zipping up her purse.

"Yep," I replied. We walked to the information desk.

Snaking our way through huddles of clueless tourists, we found an unoccupied receptionist. "Yes, hi, do you know where we can find the big end-of-school party? A ton of girls should be here for it," Mom asked.

"Yes. It is in the American Wing on the second floor," the receptionist replied, looking down at me with a smile. She opened a drawer and pulled out two blue clip-on badges that displayed an "M" with pillars on either side.

"Thank you so much!" Mom and I chimed, turning to leave.

"Jules!" I heard someone call my name. Frantically turning in a circle, trying to see where the voice came from, I spotted Annie-Beth, one of my best friends, running toward me. She slammed into me and gave me a huge hug. "Don't you look adorable? I love that dress," she exclaimed in her boisterous and playful voice.

"Hey, Annie-Beth! Thanks. I love your outfit even more!" Annie-Beth wore a white skirt with a flowing orange top and knee-high black boots. She always looked

fashionable—unlike myself. Somehow I still hadn't grad-
uated from the "adorable" clothing level to the "hip and
trendy" clothing level all my friends had already reached.
Mom didn't understand that puffy dresses weren't the
style anymore and I didn't always have to look like a
Madame Alexander doll.

"I just got here. Do you want to walk up together?"
Annie-Beth asked, looping her arm through mine. I looked
back to find Mom busily talking with Annie-Beth's mother.

"Come on!" I called. Annie-Beth pulled me along,
leading the way up a small staircase that emptied into the
Egyptian art room. The room seemed to be solid gold at
first glance: gold carpet, gold-painted walls, gold objects
inside glass boxes. I quickly looked over some ancient burial boxes and black urns painted with red paint before the
ever-energetic Annie-Beth yanked me away.

"Maddie and Samantha are already there," Annie-
Beth informed me as we crossed through an atrium and
into the Medieval Art wing. "They texted me," she added
after I gave her a confused look. The medieval art morphed
into a room full of marble statues, which morphed into a
collection of old English armor. We climbed the stairs to
the second floor and arrived in a cavernous room filled
with Monet's paintings of the lily ponds, Homer's sea-
scapes, and Mary Cassatt's paintings of beautiful young
girls. Before I could point out my favorite Impressionist
painting to Annie-Beth, we reached the American Wing.
The room was filled with a sea of familiar faces.

"Follow me," Annie-Beth said. "Samantha and Maddie
are waiting in front of *Washington Crossing the Delaware*." She
tugged my hand, whisking me around the circles of people.

"Jules! Annie-Beth! Over here," I heard my friend Samantha cry, her loud voice disturbing a rather sophisticated old man who was inspecting a bust of Andrew Jackson. She ran over to me, giving me a huge hug, her braided pigtails swinging wildly. "I can't believe you're leaving us! Why do you have to go back to Texas?"

I felt my heart flutter. I dreaded the thought of leaving my good friends. "I'm going to miss you all so much!" I said, embracing all three of my friends. A gallant George Washington loomed above us.

"Why do you have to leave now?" Maddie asked solemnly. She wore a light blue dress and a matching polka-dot headband.

"Well," I began, "Mom has been talking about leaving New York and moving back to Texas for a while now. She keeps saying, 'It's just too plumb expensive here, and I'm ready to see the expansive Texas night sky again.'" I imitated her southern accent, much to my friends' amusement.

"Where are you going to live in Texas? Are you going to rent an apartment in Dallas?" Annie-Beth asked.

"We are moving to the ranch," I said. "It's the place my mom bought in her twenties before she moved out here. I've visited there a few times, but I was so young I don't really remember anything at all."

"The ranch? You aren't going to live in the city or anything? How big is the ranch?" Samantha asked.

"Three hundred acres."

"Oh my gosh!" exclaimed Annie-Beth. "That's fifty times the size of the New York zoo!" I don't know how she knew that.

"How close is the nearest town?" Samantha asked.

"Well . . . Mom says the closest town is forty-five minutes away."

"Forty-five minutes!"

"How are you going to go shopping?"

"What if you get sick in the middle of the night? There won't be a corner market downstairs selling Advil."

"Is it true there are huge snakes in Texas?"

I blinked. "I'm . . . I'm not sure. Mom and I haven't talked about . . ." I was slowly becoming worried about ranch life.

"What happens if you get bitten by a snake in the middle of the night? I heard you can start having a reaction within thirty minutes."

"Jules, you could die!"

"I also heard the wild hog population is starting to rise in Texas. A *National Geographic* episode said that you can't outrun wild hogs. They trample you to death."

"Oh yeah, and there are a ton of scorpions there too! Texas is known for having thousands of scorpions that thrive in the heat."

"And don't forget about the coyotes. I've read that they travel in huge packs that can take down an unarmed human."

I haven't thought of any of this before.

"And how on earth are you going to get to school?"

"Are you going to have any friends? How will they come visit you?"

"Will you have a car? Or will you ride your horse to school?"

All the questions made me feel like I was slowly suffocating. Sweat began to form between my itchy dress and the skin on my neck.

"Are you going to be there all by yourself with your mom?"

Finally, a question I can answer. "Actually, the ranch hand, Beau-Dee, will still be living out there. I'm sure he can protect us from the snakes and the wild hogs and the longhorns—"

"Longhorns?" Samantha gasped.

"What are longhorns?" Annie-Beth asked.

"You know, the cows with long horns," I explained.

"Aren't those really dangerous?"

Are they dangerous?

"Are you going to have to take care of the horses all the time?" Samantha asked.

"Beau-Dee will help with that." I was growing more and more thankful for Beau-Dee by the minute.

"Aw, you'll love being with the horses," Maddie said. "Geez, I couldn't imagine being away from my pony more than a month!" Maddie had a little pony in the Hamptons that she rode every weekend.

"Well, you know what, Jules," Annie-Beth said, patting me on the shoulder. "If anyone can survive the country life, it's you." I didn't know why she thought that. Maybe it was my lack of fashion sense.

Before I could ask her, I spotted Mrs. Omega approaching me with her permanent expression of disdain. "Oh no! Hide me!" I cried, making Samantha jump. I darted behind Maddie and pretended to be very engaged in the description of Gilbert Stuart's portrait of James Monroe.

"What's wrong?" Annie-Beth exclaimed, giggling at Maddie, who was attempting to cover me like James Bond.

"Mrs. Omega's coming," I whispered through tight lips as the towering woman approached. "You know she's never liked me."

"Hello, girls. Miss Jules O'Connor, I see you have taken an interest in Gilbert Stuart," Mrs. Omega stated in a somewhat mocking tone. I turned around as if shocked to hear the schoolmarm's voice. Her sandy-white hair framed her plump face. Two beady eyes stared down at me through the windows of the black, rectangular glasses that had slipped to the tip of her unproportionally large nose.

"Yes, Stuart's portraits of the presidents are by far the most reliable. But I must say his painting of George Washington pales in comparison to Houdon's magnificent Washington sculpture," I said, hoping to shock Mrs. Omega with my knowledge of early American art. She simply nodded her head, assessing my outfit as if looking for something to complain about.

"We are sorry to hear you are moving to Texas," she said. I couldn't tell if she meant she was sorry I was leaving or sorry Texas was my final destination. "I'm sure there is some trace of culture where you are going, despite the lack of civilization." She paused. "You have enough pluck to hold your own among those rural folk. Their language is quite . . . distinct."

"I am quite looking forward to an adventure," I responded, not sure what else to say.

"Well. Best of luck." Mrs. Omega nodded her head and turned around abruptly before pretentiously walking across the room.

"What does pluck mean?" Annie-Beth asked. I wasn't sure, so I didn't respond.

"Are you okay, Jules?" Mom asked.

I stared blankly at the black leather taxi seat in front of me. I hadn't spoken since we left the museum. My mind whirled with the voices of my friends and Mrs. Omega. "Snakes . . . Reaction within thirty minutes . . . Wild hogs . . . Trampled to death . . . Scorpions . . . Thousands . . . All alone . . . Lack of civilization . . ."

"Yeah, I'm fine," I squeaked. In all actuality, I felt paralyzed. I began to think that I was going to turn into Tom Hanks in *Cast Away*, isolated in some faraway land, forced to talk to coconuts for companionship—except I would use cactus leaves.

When we arrived back at the apartment, Mom ran upstairs to get Chubbs so we could take her on her nightly walk. "You stay here," she said. "I'll be right back." Standing on the sidewalk by myself, I decided this was my last chance to absorb civilization. To my right was the tall brick church. From where I stood, I could barely make out the white steeple peeking out from behind the tall brownstone buildings. Every Sunday Mom and I had walked through those large doors. I could even remember the first, terrifying time I had walked into a room full of unfamiliar faces for Sunday school. And the time my friend Gigi and I sang with the church choir on the front steps for a Christmas celebration. It had begun to snow. *I wonder if I will ever see snow again*. Mom had made me wear an oversized red train conductor's hat so I would "stand out" in the photos. Stand out I certainly did.

To my left stood the Russian Embassy, a tall, towering building of white marble. The Russian and American flags waved from the front wall on either side of the large wooden door. Out of the corner of my eye, I looked to see if I could catch a Russian spy peering through his binoculars, watching us from across the street. Our conspiracy theorist neighbor had informed me that the FBI had an office on the tenth floor in our apartment building, so the Russian Embassy and the FBI constantly spied on each other. True to my nature, I believed the interesting story, often watching the white, antique-ish building for any signs of movement. Suddenly I saw a man looking down at me through his binoculars before suddenly darting behind the red chimney on the roof of the building . . . Or was that my imagination?

Before I could investigate further, Mom came whizzing past me, helplessly dragged by a very desperate Chubbs. It was like the Looney Tunes Road Runner: one moment Mom was beside me, and the next she was halfway down the block.

"Whoa-oa-oa-oa-oa," Mom grunted with every step as she struggled to keep her balance in her very high-heeled shoes. I couldn't help but laugh out loud. "Not-t-t funny-y-y!" Mom yelled back.

Finally, Chubbs reached the little flower box where Jack, the Polish apartment manager, was watering his three failing and wilting pansies. Jack's pet peeve, I guess you could call it, was when dogs pooped in his flower beds. So what did Chubbs do? She ran straight to the small garden and, right in front of Jack, pooped on top of his plants.

"No, no, *no!*" Jack exclaimed. "Get her out of da box! Oh no! Oh no!" He swung his watering hose in the air.

Upon seeing the water flying through the air, Chubbs cut her bathroom break short, dashed over the small wrought-iron edging, and hid behind Mom's feet, wagging her tail fervently. She looked up at Mom with her "thank you" look.

"Sorry 'bout that, Jack. But you know, we use cow poop as fertilizer back in Texas," Mom said, bending down and scooping up the poop with a lavender-scented baggy. She winked at Jack, who held his shaking head in his hands as he looked at his crushed, and now smelly, flower bed.

"Let's go say good-bye to Central Park in case we don't make it there before we leave," Mom suggested. My eyes immediately brightened. Chubbs didn't look quite as excited.

I ran ahead to the park, climbing up the steps and crossing the jogging path toward the large reservoir, dodging the many New Yorkers who looked at me like I was an irritating insect obstructing their path. Leaping toward the wrought-iron fence, I pressed my face in between the rods and gazed out across the water. Hundreds of people ran or walked around the beautiful pond, decorating the otherwise natural scene with a rainbow of colors. The setting sun cast an almost heavenly hue over the scene. *Good-bye, Central Park.*

"You know, Jules," Mom said, finally catching up with me, "your grandfather came here all the time when he was in the air force. He told me that in the wintertime, no one would come out to the reservoir except him. He would jog around here all by himself, making a path through the snow. By the time he got home, his face mask was covered in icicles!"

I don't think it's ever going to get that cold in Texas.

After a few more minutes, we returned to the apartment, crossing the busy New York streets. When we entered our building, we saw that Jackson—yet another Polish elevator operator—was now on shift.

"Halloo!" Jackson called, being his normal creepily chatty self. His blue eyes pierced through the small, round, green-rimmed glasses perched far too high up his nose.

"Hi, Jackson," Mom and I said simultaneously, though failing to match his extraordinary level of enthusiasm.

"Where have you ladies been? You look nice and sharp," Jackson said, accentuating the word *sharp* as he pulled the very rickety elevator door closed and pulled the up lever.

"Uh, just an end-of-school party," I said, shrugging it off. Jackson rolled his eyes at my dismissive tone. As the elevator slowly lifted, he looked down at Chubbs with a grimace, moving farther into the corner to avoid her tail—he had never liked Chubbs.

"Oh!" Jackson exclaimed, looking at me intently. "Let me tell you what I just read in the newspaper. It pertains to Texas . . ." He was always telling us factoids from the newspaper. "I read that Texas heat has been so bad, many people are actually dying from heatstroke! An unprecedented number of people have been hospitalized this year, and it's only June . . ."

By this time, we had reached the third floor. I dashed off before I could hear any more terrifying facts about Texas.

"But don't worry!" Jackson continued. "Texas houses have air conditioning, unlike here in the city. Good-bye now, see you tomorrow!"

"Oh, Jackson." Mom laughed once we entered the apartment. "I think he just expects us to wilt like tulips when we hit that Texas heat."

"Mom?" I asked. "Are there going to be a lot of snakes on the ranch?"

"Well, Beau-Dee said he has seen a lot of copperheads and rattlesnakes out there this year. He warned us to watch our step and keep our eyes peeled."

Oh no, Annie-Beth was right. What happens if I'm bitten and can't get to the hospital in time? I plopped down into the window seat in our living room / piano room / dining room, gazing out our large window overlooking Madison Avenue, trying to calm my nerves. Pressing my head against the window, I saw the lines and lines of tall skyscrapers that almost completely obstructed the blue sky above. An occasional taxi skidded to a stop and let people out at their various destinations. A party of five people meandered down the street, laughing obnoxiously and talking a little too loudly.

I sighed. *New York life.* I soaked in as much as I could of the beautiful street I had watched for so many years before leaning my head back against the cracked white walls and closing my eyes. As I dozed off for an afternoon nap, my mind filled with images of a Central Park full of longhorn cows.

TWO

Jules, wake up! We are almost there now," I heard Mom say. Peeling my face from the car window on which I had been leaning, I blearily opened my eyes. I blinked a few times due to the brightness of the world outside and slipped on my sunglasses. I had fallen asleep sometime during our two-and-a-half-hour drive from the airport to the ranch. Looking down at my lap, I saw Creampuff was also fast asleep in her pink polka-dot traveling kennel.

"Look!" Mom's exclamation caused me to look up with a start, bumping my forehead into the window. She pointed to a small white building. A sign reading "Creek View Community Center" hung precariously from the gutters. In the burnt patch of grass in front of the building was a yellow sign reading "Domino Night: July 2nd at 6:00."

"Isn't that cute! I remember that little community center. It's where I went to vote when I lived down here. We'll have to check out what it's like after all these years," Mom said from the driver's seat.

Rural scenes zoomed past the car: large green pastures, abnormally fat black cows, tall horses grazing on nearly invisible grass, a very small graveyard, an even smaller Baptist church, goats, chicken coops . . . and not a single house. Suddenly a beautiful lake spread out in every direction, small waves lapping at a grassy shore.

"Wow . . ." I whispered.

"The Central Park reservoir looks like a drop in a bucket now, doesn't it?" Mom said, looking at me with eyes twinkling with excitement. She was so proud of Texas. The lake disappeared and more cows and more pastures appeared behind a veil of large oak trees.

"Look, Jules. That's Sammer's house," Mom said, pointing at the first house I had seen on the road.

"Sammer?" I asked.

"Our next-door neighbor," Mom explained. I had a feeling that "next-door neighbor" no longer had the same meaning it had in New York. Five miles passed and we still had not arrived at the ranch.

Peering out the window, I saw an enormous John Deere tractor on the road in front of us, driving about fifteen miles an hour. Mom rolled down the window, sending puffs of air into the car and startling Sparkle, who sat in his leather kennel at my feet.

"Do you smell the air?"

"Yes," I answered, thrusting my head out the window. A tingle rushed through my body, a sensation that made me feel as if I was returning to a long-lost home. My hair flapped behind me wildly as I took a long, deep breath. The air smelled like trees and grasses instead of the New York exhaust and soot. Suddenly, a swarm of gnats flew into my face. I jerked my head back into the car, rubbing my hands all over my face and snorting to send the small, pesky insects out of my nose.

Finally, Mom decided to pass the tractor. As we passed, the driver waved at us with a long, slow wave. His overly tan and deeply wrinkled face was shaded by an oversized cowboy hat, and I noticed a long piece of grass sticking out from the corner of his wide smile.

"Here we are!" Mom shouted, pointing up ahead. "Oh, look, Jules! Back after all these years, and we finally get to live out here full-time. Oh, just look at it!"

A white gravel road wound its way through a field of rolling grasses and up a hill, where a windmill peeked above the lush trees at the top. The gravel crunched under the tires as Mom pulled into the entryway. On either side of the gate stood two colossal flagpoles: one bearing a ten-foot-long Texas flag and the other bearing an equally large American flag. *Everything is bigger in Texas.*

"Ah, it's so good to be home," Mom sighed. As the car strolled up the road, Chubbs began to pace in the large kennel in the back. "Can you smell the ranch, Chubbs?" Mom asked. Chubbs whined. "Oh, look, Jules! The long-horns are up!"

The car reached the top of the hill and I gasped. A large oak tree towered gallantly in the air, spreading out its innumerable branches. It was not the tree, however, that took me by surprise; it was the herd of longhorn cattle that sat in its shade. "Wow," I whispered. I had completely forgotten the majestic aura that surrounded the herd. The massive animals opened their napping eyes at the sound of our approaching vehicle. One of the longhorns stood up and began walking toward us. I had the fleeting sensation to run away from the approaching mammoth.

"Revolution!" Mom said to the white longhorn who had black ears and feet. I assumed that was the name of the cow, quickly wishing I had also studied Mom's "Book of Longhorn Names." Revolution stopped and stared at us, seeming to evaluate whether we were friend or foe, her dark eyes glistening in the harsh Texas sunlight. I almost exclaimed out loud as a second longhorn stood up from his napping position under the tree and assumed his post beside Revolution. No joke, this . . . giant . . . was as tall as our SUV, and the span of his horns exceeded the width of our car. Despite the alarming size, I couldn't help but appreciate his beautiful markings: the colors around his eyes reminded me of Elizabeth Taylor's makeup in *Cleopatra*.

"Valentino!" Mom called. "That is the steer I was telling you about, Jules. The one Grandpa picked up when he was a little calf. Oh, Valentino, do you remember when Dad picked you up as a baby?" I could hardly imagine that the colossus was ever small enough to lift from the ground. Mom was about to explain something else when an oversized pickup truck came barreling around the bend in the gravel road. It came so quickly I feared it was going to hit us, but it veered off the road and into the grass just in time, pulling up on my side of the car.

"Oh, it's you!" A strapping man in his late thirties peered down from his truck window. He looked just like Matthew McConaughey, except with shaggy brown hair and light blue eyes. "Good Lord, I thought you were a robber. I had my hand on my pistol, ready to blow out your tires!"

"Beau-Dee!" Mom exclaimed. *Thank heaven above for Beau-Dee.*

"Hey there, Emily! My, my, Jules, you've grown up faster than a beanstalk."

I smiled proudly, craning my neck to look up at Beau-Dee through my car window.

"How are you?" Mom asked, shouting across me.

"Fair to middlin'. Yourself?" Beau-Dee asked, resituating his baseball cap.

"Fantastic! It is so great to be back after all this time. I was just showing Jules the longhorns," Mom stated.

"Yeah, the longhorns are quite a sight, ain't they? Um, hey, Emily . . ."

"Mm-hm," Mom replied, distracted by the beauty of the longhorn herd.

"So I got another job in town and . . . since it is too long of a drive from here every mornin', I'm plannin' on leavin'. Actually, I've technically already left. The movers came and loaded up my stuff before you got here, but I've been waitin' to leave till I could tell you face-to-face."

My stomach sank to my feet. It seemed as if Beau-Dee's pickup truck suddenly cast a dark shadow over our car.

"Wait, hold on," Mom said, suddenly directing all of her attention to Beau-Dee. She tweaked her glasses unnecessarily. "You're leaving?"

"Mm-hm."

"Wait . . . you . . . When?"

"Tomorrow. Just got one more box to pack."

"Tomorrow? Beau-Dee, I kind of need more than a day's notice."

"Well, I didn't want to bother y'all with it during your travels, and the job wasn't confirmed until late last week. I wanted to wait and tell you till I was sure of everythin'."

Mom leaned forward, coughing twice, and began to drink some water. I knew that meant her heart was palpitating. My uncle Tom had told her to cough and drink some water to stop the palpitations—Mom claimed it worked.

"Well, Beau-Dee, um . . . ," Mom said. "I'm sad to see you leave after all these years . . . on such late notice."

I didn't feel that "sad" fully quantified our emotions.

"Thanks, Emily. Well, I'll leave y'all with your longhorns," Beau-Dee began, the car engine restarting with a roar. "I was just fixin' to go into town and buy some more feed for the horses. I'll see y'all later tonight. I got to teach y'all how to feed all the critters!" Beau-Dee drove off, waving as he went, leaving us in a cloud of diesel smoke.

There was a long pause inside the car. Mom was practicing her deep-breathing exercises. A grasshopper the size of my palm flew onto the windshield, its beady eyes just inches from my face. I jumped in my seat, quickly rolling up my window in case it decided to take off again. *I didn't know grasshoppers could get that big.*

I looked over at Mom, who stared out the windshield into space. She repeatedly ran her fingers through her hair. I wasn't sure if I should speak or not, but I had a burning question. "Mom?" I whispered. Mom didn't respond. "Mom?"

Mom sighed. "Yeah?"

"What are we going to do?"

"Well." Mom didn't speak—or move—for what felt like an eternity. Then she looked at me with a determined, mischievous look in her eye. "We are just going to have to take care of the ranch ourselves now!" Mom whooped like a coyote—a very sudden change of attitude.

"What?" I exclaimed.

Now who is going to protect us from the coyotes?

Who is going to rescue us from a stampeding pack of wild hogs?

What if Mom is bitten by a snake in the middle of the night and has to go to the hospital . . . Who is going to drive us?

"Are we going to look for someone else to help us?" I asked, holding on to one last strand of hope.

"Why would we? Oh, we can do it ourselves! We'll like the privacy. Heck, now we can walk down to the barn in our nightgowns if we want. No one will be able to see us for miles . . ."

Oh my gosh, we're going to be out here all alone, miles and miles away from any human contact.

"We can feed the horses morning and night, we can give the cows their cubes three times a week, and we can drive around the ranch in the four-wheeler to check on things . . ."

Annie-Beth was right. I could die out here in the middle of nowhere and no one would even know it. Mom attempted to move the car forward, but Revolution blocked the road, staring at me with unnatural intensity. She slowly, intently chewed a piece of grass that dangled from her mouth.

"It won't be bad at all! It will be fun. It will be an adventure, Jules!"

I sat immobilized, unable to talk. Beau-Dee was my last hope. Beau-Dee was now leaving.

"How many longhorns do we have again?" I finally asked.

"Twenty-five right now, but Beau-Dee said last week that we are having a lot of babies right now."

I blinked. Revolution was *still* staring at me. "And the ranch is . . .?"

"Three hundred acres."

"Okay," I squeaked.

Mom appeared not to hear me. "Let's drop Creampuff, Sparkle, and Chubbs off at the house before we go down to the barn. And you have to change!" Mom added suddenly, looking at my outfit. I wore the only stylish outfit I owned: a little blue skirt and a white shirt with white sandals. My grandmother had purchased it for me. "You can't go walking around the ranch in that outfit! You have to wear jeans and boots on a ranch. Remember, we have to look out for the snakes."

Mom steered the car into the driveway, which was canopied with trees. No garage here—just tree cover. Mom killed the ignition and opened her door. A cacophony of dog barks roared from behind a crooked and very uneven white picket fence encircling the house. The two-story structure emerged from the surrounding trees, reminding me of a little bird's nest tucked away in the deep folds of branches. It was a small house, no more than twelve hundred square feet according to my grandmother—who would know, because she's a Realtor.

Chubbs barked from the backseat. "Coming, Chubbs!" I shouted. Before jumping out of the car, I carefully inspected the gravel road for any signs of movement. Finding none, I walked to the back of the vehicle. Mom had already opened the hatch, prepared to lower Chubbs's oversized kennel.

"Ready?" Mom asked, holding on to one side of the kennel. I nodded, white-knuckling the kennel handle. "One . . . two . . . three." The kennel lurched into the air, my arm muscles spontaneously combusting into fiery pain. My unathletic, citified body had no idea how to handle real physical exertion.

A slightly dizzy Chubbs bounded out of the kennel and ran to the fence.

"Hey, guys!" Mom greeted the three dogs awaiting us. As we opened the gate, an elegant red dog bowed down at our feet, tucking her head between her front paws.

"Jessie!" Mom said, kneeling down and hugging the little dog. Despite her exceedingly white face, which revealed her old age, her golden-red coat glistened over her strong but petite body. She looked at me over Mom's shoulder with highly intelligent, dark, sparkling eyes, her white-tipped tail wagging rapidly.

Suddenly, a huge black blob started running toward me and jumped, placing his paws firmly on my shoulders. "Ah!" I cried, falling backward into the yard. A large dog snout loomed over my face and began licking my nose.

"That must be General," Mom said. Beau-Dee had sent word to us that he had found a sweet black lab on the side of the road. We had instructed him to keep the dog for us as long as he got along with the other dogs. He obviously had. General sat down on top of me but quickly rolled off onto his back, asking me to rub his tummy. "Hey there, General, aren't you a good boy?"

A husky, croaking bark came from behind me. Turning my head, I saw a hulky black-and-white dog who reminded me of Cousin Itt from *The Addams Family*. He walked over, placed his paw on my leg in greeting, then looked up at me with large round eyes. "That's Buster, Jessie's son," Mom said. "He was born the same year as you." He looked absolutely nothing like Jessie.

We finally made it to the door, but before I could enter my new home—still lacking our boxes—all of the dogs burst through the doorway, nearly knocking the door out, collapsing onto the cool, air-conditioned floor.

"Our little cottage!" Mom said, closing the door behind her. "Now, let's not look around yet. We have to hurry up and get back outside so we can go see the horses. I packed some ranch clothes for us in my carry-on bag . . ." Sparkle meowed from his kennel, which was at Mom's feet. "Hold on, Sparky." She handed me a pair of jeans and a T-shirt. "Here, put this on and pick out a pair of boots from under the stairs. There should be some old ones there in a big basket. I'm going to put Creampuff and Sparkle upstairs."

After throwing on the clothes, I carefully folded my one stylish outfit and gathered my hair back in a ponytail before searching under the stairs for boots. I spotted the old, tiny red cowboy boots I had worn the last time I was out here. After finding a suitable pair of cowboy boots, I slipped them on and walked to the door. Mom was there waiting.

"You can't wear those!" Mom exclaimed, pointing to the pair I had on my feet.

"Why not?" *I thought cowboy boots were the shoe of choice for ranch work.*

"Remember what I said about the copperheads and snakes? Well . . ." Mom walked by me and looked under the stairs, searching for another pair. She emerged seconds later carrying the most atrocious pair of lace-up boots I had ever seen in my whole life. They were camouflage print and looked about ten sizes too big for me. "These are protective snake boots. If a snake bites your foot, it can't bite through this boot, so you're safe. Just put on an extra layer of socks and they should fit," Mom said, plopping the huge boots down on the floor. With much heaving and pulling, I finally forced my foot into the boot.

"Now, you ready?" Mom asked, after seeing I had double knotted the laces on the boots. I nodded and waddled outside, quite unsure what I was supposed to be ready for.

We exited the yard and emerged onto the white gravel road. A little distance down, on the left side of the road, stood a blue barn with a white roof. I smiled. The view looked like one of Winslow Homer's paintings I had seen in the Met.

"See this ranch, Jules?" Mom asked, stopping mid-stride. I stopped beside her and followed her hand with my eyes as she waved it slowly across the horizon. "Mockingbird Hill! Do you know why I named it that?" Mom asked. She didn't pause for me to answer. "I purchased this ranch with the money I earned from my first *New York Times* best-selling book. And, as you know, my favorite novel is *To Kill a Mockingbird*, and since the state bird of Texas is the mockingbird, I found the name quite fitting. Mockingbird Hill.

"When I bought this land, there wasn't anything here: no electricity, no piped water, no fences, no barn, no riding arena, no house. I drew it all on a dinner napkin one day—where I wanted the arena to be and how I wanted the barn to look. The first thing I built was the barn for Maggie. I didn't even think about a house for myself until she had a place to stay.

"I've always wanted to live out here, but I moved to New York to restart my writing career . . . find new inspiration. Now, finally, we get to live out here all the time! Our three-hundred-acre ranch. So much that hasn't been discovered yet!"

I was already feeling the effects of the sweltering Texas heat—I even thought I felt my skin turning crispy. Somehow Mom wasn't fazed by the heat; she was speed-walking down to the barn. I decided I'd better follow her closely instead of risk being gored by a longhorn.

I looked up to find one solitary, dry-looking white cloud in the sky. It cast no shade. Hawks with red tails and small scissortail birds swooped in and around the huge oak trees; vultures with their red turkey heads and ragged, expansive wings soared and peered down to the ground far below. They looked so massive compared to the puny pigeons in the city. Large yellow flowers with black centers waved at me in the wind. Much to my surprise, these flowers were still in the ground and not in a flower stand like the ones at Mr. and Mrs. Choi's market in New York.

Suddenly, I lost my balance, almost falling flat on my back as the ground moved out from beneath me. After regaining my balance, I looked around, trying to determine what on God's green earth had just happened. *Was it an earthquake?*

"Oh my gosh!" I shouted, seeing a huge mound of poop in the middle of the road was now stamped with my footprint. "Ew!" I cried. "Is that what I think it is?"

"A cow patty," Mom said nonchalantly.

"A cow what?" I asked in anguish. I began running around in the grass, dragging my shoe, trying to rid myself of the toxic smell. It was to no avail; flies were beginning to follow me, tracking the smell of poop. But these flies were not the New York flies; these were Texas flies, ten times larger and five times as aggressive. I felt like Pigpen from *Peanuts*, except I was surrounded by flies instead of dust. I reluctantly resumed the walk to the barn, this time watching my steps.

When we arrived at the barn, a chorus of neighs and whinnies greeted us. Sunlight beamed in through the enormous door in the back, bouncing off the red rafters that held up the wooden stalls. Flies zoomed through the air like small fighter jets looking to land. In the first stall on my left was a tall black horse. A little sign reading "Rocky" hung from his door. Mom always told me he was a famous horse, since he had starred in movies.

"Howdy, Rocky!" Mom called, walking into his stall. She embraced Rocky's neck in her arms. "He always makes me feel better. He is like a therapy horse. Aren't you, Rocky boy? Mm-hm." As she held on to his arching neck, she took a deep breath, her shoulders lowering and her face growing peaceful and serene. I didn't feel brave enough to close my eyes around such a large horse, so I stood in the entrance to the stall. But I could tell what Mom was talking about. Rocky looked sweetly at me—his soul seemed to talk to mine and assuage all my worries.

The stall across from Rocky's was full of hay. Bales and bales and bales of hay climbed all the way to the top of the barn. *How am I ever going to be able to reach all that hay now that Beau-Dee is gone?* I thought all the stalls on that side of the barn were vacant until I saw a little black nose pop out from above the stall door in the middle of the barn.

"Jules, there's R2!" Mom shouted, looking over my shoulder at the little black nose. Mom's best friend was a horse trainer, and when I turned two years old—even though we lived in New York—she gave me a genuine Texas gift: a pony. I had been instructed to name the pony, and due to my strange obsession with the Star Wars movies, and particularly the little droid R2-D2, I named the mysterious creature R2.

I walked over to her stall. "Hey, girl," I whispered as I stroked her dark brown coat. She was all one color except for a white streak on her nose and two white socks on her back feet. She whinnied loudly in response.

"Maggie May! My sweet girl!" Mom's voice echoed throughout the barn as she walked to the next stall. And there she was: the most beautiful palomino horse I had ever seen, her coat as vibrant as a gate of pure gold but as varied as the grains of sand on the seashore, her mane as thick as it was long, her tail rippling as she shooed the flies. But it was her eyes that amazed me; they were so clear, so real. Maggie let out a rich, deep-throated nicker and dipped her head into Mom's chest, nuzzling her in greeting. It was such a sweet sight, Mom and Maggie connecting like that, like human to human.

"Hi, Maggie," I said, walking over to her in awe. Maggie had a royal air about her.

"Jules, let's go take a ride on the trail to the North Forty!" Mom said. I stopped dead in my tracks.

"Um, really?" The thought of a trail ride sent butterflies into my stomach. *How am I supposed to control a five-hundred-pound animal while helplessly riding on its back through uncharted woods?*

"Yeah! Why not?"

"All right, if you want to," I said as my eyebrows cocked in concern.

"It will be so fun! I haven't ridden in forever!" Mom said. Mom grabbed a blue halter that hung on Maggie's stall door. As if thoroughly understanding the situation, Maggie lowered her head so that Mom could easily secure the halter over her face. "I'm going to get a brush so we can groom her before we ride."

I walked over to stand by Maggie and wrapped my arms around her neck. Maggie nuzzled my side. "You smell so sweet, Maggie," I told her after taking a big whiff of her natural perfume. Her skin quivered under my hand as I traced my finger through her coat.

"I've wanted to make a perfume that smells like her," Mom responded. I could just imagine a perfume seller telling a customer in Bergdorf Goodman, "This is the latest scent from Texas, called Maggie the Horse." That would never fly.

After Mom finished brushing Maggie, she placed a large leather saddle onto the horse's back. "Now"— Mom sighed after making final adjustments to Maggie's saddle—"let's saddle R2. Do you think you can do it by yourself?" I nodded.

"This thing is heavy." I zigzagged across the barn floor, attempting to balance the mountain of saddle and bridle I held in my twisted arms. Since I could barely see where I was walking, I repeatedly stepped on the bridle, which trailed behind me like the train of Maria's wedding gown in *The Sound of Music*. Carrying my book bag up seven flights of stairs every morning to get to my classroom in New York seemed like a walk in the park compared to this.

Mom walked R2 out of her stall and helped me situate the saddle on her back. R2 seemed quite perturbed. Soon we were walking out of the barn, prepared to embark on our adventure.

Mom hoisted herself into the air, as if flying, and landed on Maggie's back. "Can you mount R2 by yourself?" she asked. I looked at Mom with wide eyes, then looked at little R2, back at Mom, back at R2. The pony was no taller than my chest, and I thought it would be very embarrassing if I was unable to mount such a small horse.

"I can do it," I said out of pride. I threw R2's reins over her neck and tried to jump on. My abdomen slammed into the horn on the saddle and I flew backward onto the ground, scraping my hands. *I cannot breathe. I think I broke a rib. I didn't even last one day.*

"Jules, stop, hold on," Mom said, hopping off Maggie and lifting me to my feet. "You have to hold on to the reins while you mount her so she doesn't take off, first of all. Then you grab the horn with the same hand, put your left foot in the stirrup, and then swing the other leg over."

Following Mom's directions, I finally mounted R2. I felt very proud of my accomplishment.

And we were off. Mom led the way as I struggled to keep up. R2 kept attempting to make a U-turn back to the barn. I had absolutely no control over the creature. I attempted to pull the reins, but R2 started walking in a circle instead, completely ignoring my commands. Midcircle, R2 decided she wanted to eat some of the grass from the trail, yanking her head down and taking my arm with it.

"R2, are you trying to dislocate my shoulder?" I rubbed my shoulder, then pulled at the reins until she finally stopped tearing at the grass. She still wouldn't walk forward.

"Are you all right back there?" Mom asked, looking over her shoulder, way ahead of me on gallant and well-trained Maggie.

"Sure," I said, pulling once more on the reins, sending R2's head flying up, her mouth draped in grass.

"Kick her in the ribs like this," Mom said, pressing the heel of her boot into Maggie's side. Maggie began to walk at once. I mirrored Mom's actions and R2 jolted forward. We walked calmly for a while, the leather saddle squeaking as R2's belly swayed back and forth with each step.

Up ahead, the trail opened into a large pasture Mom called the "North Forty."

"Come on, let's ride around a little in here!"

"What do you mean?" I asked. "I thought that was what we've been doing this whole time."

"No, like this," Mom said. With the kick of Mom's boot, Maggie took off racing through the pasture. Mom's hair and Maggie's golden tail flew back in the wind. "Yeehaw!" Mom screamed. Mom and Maggie slowly shrank as they ran to the far side of the pasture before turning around and slowly growing larger again. I just sat on the immobilized R2. She was once again eating grass.

"Isn't this great?" Mom shouted as Maggie looped around behind me and took off again. It did look exhilarating to ride a horse like that, free from everything, not a care in the world.

I took a deep breath. Another deep breath. *You can do this.* I kicked R2 twice with all my might.

Nothing happened.

I tried again. Kick. Kick.

Nothing happened.

"Argh! R2, come on!" I said through clenched teeth, kicking side to side furiously. R2 remained immobile, nose to the ground, eating.

Then, as if a lightbulb went off in her head, she darted off, full speed ahead.

"Help!" I screamed. R2 ran so quickly I felt my body begin to fly backward. I held on to the reins for dear life. "Stop, R2, stop!" *I'm going to die!*

"Jules, say 'Whoa!'" Mom yelled at me.

"Whoa!" I yelled into R2's ear as my palms became abnormally sweaty. At that command she skidded to a screeching halt. Dust circled around me like a typhoon. I tried to cough up the dust plugging my airway.

"You okay?" Mom asked, riding up to me on Maggie.

"Oh yeah, just fine. Just fine," I coughed.

Mom took off again and I walked R2 underneath a mammoth cedar tree and into much-appreciated shade. To my right, a beautiful blue pond dotted the pasture. Robins flew down to drink some of the water before flying back up into the high branches of the trees.

"Jules!" Mom cried. I looked up to find Mom. She and Maggie were heading my direction, but I could tell something was wrong. Mom's face was riddled with angst. The saddle was slowly sliding to the right, taking Mom with it.

"Whoa, Maggie, whoa!" Mom cried. Maggie appeared not to hear and continued on.

Mom tried to pull Maggie to a halt, but she was already falling off. Furiously kicking her legs, Mom tried to free her feet from the stirrups, yet they seemed to be stuck. After one large kick, Mom's feet slid from the stirrups at last and she tumbled off, her head banging against the hard ground.

"Mom!" I yelled. I sprang off R2, running to Mom, who sat holding the side of her head with her hands. Maggie had stopped and looked absolutely terrified. Mom's glasses were crooked and dangled from one ear. "Mom! Mom, are you okay? Talk to me, Mom!" I cried. *Where's Beau-Dee when I need him?*

"Shh, shh, I'm okay, I'm okay! Where is Maggie?" Mom mumbled. I pointed to where Maggie stood, quivering uncontrollably with the saddle now under her belly. Mom got up and began walking slowly over to Maggie.

"It's okay, Maggie, it's okay. Shh, calm down. The saddle just slipped. It's okay," Mom cooed. Mom was just about to lay her hand on the reins when Maggie took off, full speed. She ran by an oblivious R2 and was gone.

"Oh no!" Mom said, attempting to run after Maggie. "Where is she going? We may never find her."

"We have to go find her!" I said, running to remount R2. Mom helped me onto the stubborn pony and quickly led us back to the trail to the barn. Suddenly, I saw Maggie running toward us, the saddle banging against her belly.

"Mom, there she is!" I pointed in front of me to the golden blob barreling toward us.

"Maggie, stop, stop!" Mom yelled. Maggie, however, did not stop and kept running and running. "Oh, geez! She is never going to calm down as long as that saddle keeps hitting her side. Oh, what are we going to do?"

I had no idea.

"Wait here for a second," Mom said, walking off the trail to search around. "Maggie!" Her loud voice echoed through the forest. I looked around in a 360, hoping to catch a glimpse of Maggie. Nothing.

R2, on the other hand, no longer attempted to eat and instead just hung her head so her nose brushed the top of the grass. I looked down at the grass beneath me, finding one solitary flower—it was probably a weed. But it was so pretty: blue with a white center. As I inspected the beautiful weed, I realized that it gradually grew closer and closer to my face. *How strange,* I thought. *It appears the flower is getting larger and larger as I'm watching it.*

"Holy Moses! Jules, get off!" Mom suddenly yelled. I frantically looked around in shock. "R2 is lying down, Jules. Get off now!" Not knowing what else to do, I leaped off R2 and tumbled onto the ground just before the pony plopped onto the ground as well. For some reason, R2 had decided to take an impromptu nap.

"Is this normal?" I asked. Maddie had never told me about her pony taking a sudden nap in the middle of a ride.

"Nope. I think R2 is just plumb tuckered out," Mom sighed.

After much heaving and pushing, Mom and I were finally able to get R2 back onto her feet. "Come on, come on," Mom urged, "we have to find Maggie." Mom led us at a fast pace, and we were quickly back at the barn.

"Maggie!" I exclaimed. She stood in the barn right in front of Rocky's stall, trembling all over and lathered in white, foaming sweat.

"Maggie, I was so worried!" Mom ran to her beloved horse, who seemed too tired to move. "You smart girl, coming back to the barn. Good girl."

"I'd call this an exhausting day," I said, collapsing into a white rocking chair after unsaddling R2 and putting her back in her stall. "And it's only one o'clock!"

"Do you want a shower, Maggie May?" Mom asked. She unsaddled Maggie and led her out of the barn to the water hose. "You coming?" she asked me.

"I'm very happy here," I answered, closing my eyes, letting the large overhead fan inside the barn dry the sweat that plastered my face.

Quickly becoming bored with inaction, I walked over to Rocky's stall and began discussing everything that happened on the trail ride. Rocky seemed very interested in the story and listened attentively. Just then, I saw something move out of the corner of my eye. I spun around and faced the barn wall.

"*MO-O-O-O-O-M!*" I yelled at the top of my lungs. I ran out to the middle of the gravel road, running straight into Mom.

"What?" Mom screamed at me.

"There's a . . . it's a . . . really big . . ." I was hyperventilating.

"Spit it out!"

"Snake!"

"A snake?"

"Big snake, *really big* snake. Lying on the rafters in the barn." I flailed my arms around, trying to describe the length of the five-foot-long snake I had seen hiding along the barn wall. Voldemort's Nagini had nothing on this snake.

Mom whipped her cell phone from her jeans pocket and slammed it against her cheek. Sweat suctioned the screen to her face. I didn't know who she was calling, but all I could think about was that snake slithering around the rafters. I sporadically checked over my shoulder, expecting to find it behind me, bearing its fangs.

"Sammer? It's Emily."

"Howdy, Emily. Are y'all here yet?" I heard Sammer's voice on the other side of the line.

"Oh yeah, we're home, but . . . Well, we need you to come over, like now. Are you home?" Mom asked a little frantically.

"I'm home. What's the matter?" he said really slowly.

"Well, there is a huge snake in our barn, and it might be heading toward our horses," Mom said quickly and urgently.

"Well, that isn't good now, is it?" Sammer said. "I'll be right over."

"Thanks," Mom said, hanging up the phone. I stared at Mom with wide eyes. "It's okay. Just stand out here with me and everything will be all right."

Sammer was over in a jiffy, speeding down the road in a four-wheeler, swinging a rifle with his left hand as he drove with his right.

"Here I come, you snake! You can't mess with me!" Sammer yelled, honking the horn as he drove, a line of dust trailing his path. Gravel swirled around him like a tornado as he skidded to a halt in front of us. Sammer was a sight to behold: a six-foot-two, muscular figure donned in navy overalls, a bright orange T-shirt, a cowboy hat, and alligator-skin cowboy boots. He cocked his gun.

Before Sammer could exit his four-wheeler, Beau-Dee's pickup truck came roaring up to the barn. "What's all the commotion?" he asked.

"There's a huge snake!" I yelled.

"Snake?" Beau-Dee asked. He whipped his hand to the holster hanging from his belt then pulled out and cocked his silver pistol. "Where is it?" He ran toward us, waving his gun around, searching for the snake.

I'm going to be splat in the middle of a Wild West shoot-out!

"Ah!" I screamed. This was all too much. I quickly practiced my duck-and-roll skills. Every roll felt like I was rolling over rocks—wait, I was. I stopped rolling when I felt the gravel change into grass and landed right in the middle of a patch of sticker burs. All I wanted was a shower—my old, rusty, inept New York shower, even if it did flood my bathroom.

"Don't shoot!" Mom screamed, throwing up her arms.

"I wasn't going to shoot y'all!" Beau-Dee cried, skidding to a halt beside Mom.

"I ain't gonna shoot nobody! I'm gonna shoot that there snake!" Sammer said as he fired his gun into the air. I was still, dead still, in the middle of the bur patch. I couldn't see anybody or anything and had no clue what was going on. My field of vision consisted of blue sky and more blue sky.

"What in the world!" I yelped, hoping no one had been shot. I must have sounded like a rabid coyote, because Sammer swung his rifle around, pointing it right at me. My eyes stared straight into the gun barrel. "Don't shoot! Don't shoot! Don't . . . shoot," I said, feeling a little bit light-headed.

"You know by the time y'all git finished with all this hoopla, the snake's gonna be long gone," Sammer said.

"Please, just don't use any guns," Mom said.

"All right," Beau-Dee and Sammer said simultaneously. Sammer walked back to his four-wheeler and returned his gun to his gun rack. He then pulled out a big silver rod.

"What is that for?" I asked warily while trying to detach the pointy, sticky thorns from my skin and clothes.

"To git that snake from the wall!" Sammer said, swinging the rod and walking quickly to the barn like he was the undisputed king of all snake catchers.

"Jules, go sit up there at the top of the hill until I say you can come down," Mom said with a worried, snake-phobic/gun-phobic look on her face. I limped to the top of the gravel road about twenty feet from the barn—hardly a hill by any stretch of the imagination—and sat down on the scalding gravel rocks. An inchworm slowly made its way across a piece of gravel to my right. After a while, Mom came up and sat by me.

"What's going on? What kind of snake is it? Is it poisonous? Is Sammer getting it?" I flooded Mom with all my questions, forgetting about the inchworm.

"Sammer is trying to get the snake. I don't know anything else," Mom said.

I turned my attention back to the inchworm, yet I was unable to find it. "Yikes!" I exclaimed, jumping two feet off the ground upon finding the inchworm now on my leg. "How did you get there?" I asked the little green worm as I removed it from my leg. "Oh, look, there's Sammer! He has the snake."

"Stay here," Mom said, wearily standing up. "What kind of snake is it?" Mom yelled from the top of the hill.

"He's a li'l chick'n snake."

"A what?"

"A *chicken* snake. It's perfectly harmless and will eat all them rats that're in your feed room." Sammer said. "Come o'er here and touch him."

Eager to obey the man with access to a big gun, I began to stand up. Before I could do so, however, Mom piped up, "No, we're okay! Thank you, though," and pushed me back into a sitting position.

"Oh, come on, Emily," Sammer said. "Don't be chick'n."

"Nope," Mom said.

"Jules, you come o'er here and touch him!"

"O-o-okay!" I said. As I started to walk over, Mom grasped my hand, nearly cutting off the circulation to my finger. I tried to pry myself loose from Mom's death grip, but it was no use, so I just started to walk oh so very slowly down the hill, dragging poor Mom behind me.

"I don't got all day, Emily," Sammer said. "I gotta get to work on the railroad."

Once I got to the bottom of the "hill," I went over to Sammer and the snake. The snake's tongue flickered out of its mouth. I was very relieved to find that Sammer was holding the snake's head between his thumb and forefinger, keeping its jaws closed. I almost felt bad for the reptile—it looked so uncomfortable with its face all squished and scrunched up in between Sammer's massive, strong fingers. It must have wondered why in the world it had decided to come out of its comfy hole in the wall and why it was now out here in the hot, muggy sun. Flipping its tail viciously, the snake almost skinned the front of my legs.

"Okay, let's get this over with. Touch it and let's get away from it," Mom told me, nervously.

I reached out my hand and stroked the top of his head. It was rough, cool, and leathery. It felt . . . like a reptile.

I reached out to touch it again, but Mom tugged on my arm, sending me flying backward a few steps. She started pulling me back up the hill, not taking her eyes off the snake, which was still in striking range.

"Thank you for coming to our rescue, Sammer," Mom said.

"Now *you* have to come o'er here and touch him, Emily."

Poor ol' Mom. She let go of my hand and stomped right on over to that snake, stopping about two feet away. Then she stretched out her hand and tapped it on the head.

"Happy now, Sammer?" Mom asked.

Sammer simply nodded, hurling the snake into the forest.

At that moment, I didn't know who I felt worse for: Mom, who just had to rise above her snake phobia, or the snake, who was taken from its home—where it was probably born—only to have its head squished and touched by two people, and then, as the grand finale to its horrible day, be thrown seven feet into the air and flung into thornbushes. I ended up going with the snake.

Three

To celebrate our first Fourth of July back from New York City, Mom and I decided to throw a party. We miraculously had almost all of our billions of boxes unpacked and our house looked halfway normal. Give or take a little, as all of our pictures were still perched against the walls or in chairs, and my desk still had moving wrap around it.

Mom had set some lawn chairs out on the grass, as well as one of our foldout tables. We even purchased a little flag-patterned umbrella from the Twisted Cactus Convenience Store in town to try to hide a very special guest from the ever-present sun—my grandmother, Mimi. Mimi, of course, had invited herself because she "knew we would need help." So that was why, on July 4th, I saw a white Mercedes pull up in our driveway . . . three hours early.

"Hi, Jules!" Mimi sang joyously as she pranced through the gate of our yard.

"Oh! Hi, Mimi. My, you look festive," I said, giving her a hug. She wore a bright blue shirt with red-and-white-striped chiffon sleeves. But it was the hair ornament that caught my attention. She wore antlers that had "July 4" running across them and streamers on either side of her Marilyn Monroe hairdo.

"Oh, well, you know me! I always have to be in the spirit of the season. Wait, that's Christmas. Ha-ha! Oh well," she said, laughing. "Would you mind helping me and Grandpa unload all the goodies I brought?"

"Grandpa came?" I asked, shocked. He was a very mellow man. His favorite place in the world was his La-Z-Boy chair alongside his dog, Buster (not to be confused with my Buster), and his "feral" cat, Meow. He was rarely allowed this luxury, however, due to Mimi's dog allergy—she always tried to keep a distance from Buster's dog hair.

"Yes, I was able to pry Grandpa from the Rangers baseball game. He isn't in the best of spirits, but at least he's here. That's a miracle in and of itself!" Mimi said, opening the door to the house. That was true—Grandpa was definitely not as festively minded and outgoing as Mimi, and it took a lot of begging and crossing all your toes and holding your breath at all the right times to get him to a party.

"Well, hello, Mother," I heard Mom say from the front porch as Mimi walked to the house. "You're awfully early." I cringed, remembering I had forgotten to inform Mom that Mimi was planning on coming this early. In my defense, Mimi had informed me when she was already on the way, so there wasn't anything I could have done about it anyway.

I walked over to the back of Mimi's car and noticed her license plate glimmering in the sun: "HOMES" in bold black letters. She was, after all, the "number one Realtor in the Metroplex," and deserving of her license plate. I found Grandpa bent over, trying to retrieve a grocery bag from the backseat.

"Grandpa! I'm so glad you came," I said excitedly, running over to him.

"Hi, Jules," he said, holding his glasses in his mouth. He stood up straight and gave me a huge bear hug.

"What do you need help with?" I asked, peeking into the car. "Oh my," I added, seeing gazillions of bags from the 99¢ Only Store.

"Mimi went a little crazy and bought the whole place. It was disastrous. And she used my credit card," Grandpa said, looking at me from the corner of his eye.

"Yes, I went a little crazy, but I did not buy the whole store," Mimi said, approaching the car quickly. "I mean, I had to buy the Texas-shaped ice cube trays, right?"

I laughed and picked up a couple of bags.

"Come on, Maurice, what are you waiting for? My hair is falling in this heat," Mimi said to Grandpa, who was slowly tucking his glasses into the front of his shirt. Mimi tugged out a big Neiman Marcus shopping bag and handed it to Grandpa.

"What's in that?" I asked, becoming a little worried that people were arriving in three short hours. We now had a load of unexpected decorations to display.

"Oh, this? My new July Fourth platters," Mimi said from inside the car.

"Good Lord, Lorraine!" Grandpa said as he looked inside the bag. "Did I pay for this?"

"Yes," Mimi said, closing the car door with her hip and carrying three shopping bags toward the house. "I love you too!"

I suppressed a full-blown laugh attack and ended up resembling a sputtering fool. "Did you swallow a fly?" Mimi asked as she walked beside me.

"No, no, I'm fine!" I said, glancing back at Grandpa, who was still looking inside the bag as he walked. I hoped he wouldn't find the receipt before the party was over. He looked up at me with his trademark half smile.

"Holy Moses, Mother! I hope this is all going home with you," Mom said as we walked in the door of the cool, air-conditioned house. "I just finished unpacking one hundred and one boxes, and I can tell you no new item is wanted in this house."

"I can take everything home, but I'd thought you might like to keep it," Mimi said as she unloaded the platters onto the kitchen table. It was the most amazing set I had ever seen. The bean bowl was a hollowed-out "4," the lettuce dish had fireworks on the bottom, the coleslaw dish was a colonial hat, and the burger-and-hot-dog platter had "July 4th" in a bold red font with multicolored fireworks.

"That is awfully cute," I said, my eyes huge.

"Well, I'm glad somebody likes it," Mimi said, folding up the bag.

"I need to sit down," Grandpa said.

"Are you okay, Dad?" Mom asked, turning her head from the sink, where she was cleaning our freshly unpacked party cups.

"Yeah, it's just bloody hot out there!" he said. I ran to the fridge and opened an ice-cold Diet Coke for him. He loved Diet Coke.

"Here."

"Thank you, sweetheart."

"Hell's bells! What is that?" Mimi exclaimed, pointing to something that was right beside the door.

"What?" Mom, Grandpa, and I all exclaimed at the same time.

Oh, please don't be a snake. Mimi will not take that well.

"It . . . it . . . looks like a . . . ," Mimi began.

"Oh, for Pete's sake! Just spit it out," Mom said. I burst out laughing when I saw what Mimi was pointing at. It was, simply, a fluffy wad of gold and black dog hair.

"Mimi, it's a dust bunny. It won't hurt you; it isn't even living," I said, picking it up and walking over to the trash can.

"We can't have guests over with your floor looking like this!" Mimi exclaimed. "And have you no consideration for my allergies? You know I can't be in a haven of dog hair!" she added, marching over to the laundry room. I looked at Grandpa and we exchanged a roll of the eyes.

"Mother, you know we have been a little bit busy unpacking boxes. I was going to vacuum after I finished scrubbing these party cups," Mom began. She looked at me from the sink. She had a towel draped over her shoulder and her hands were covered in suds. Several strands of hair were falling from her short ponytail. "I just vacuumed yesterday, and—"

"Where is your vacuum, Emily?" Mimi asked as she opened the closet under the stairs. "Who can find anything in this mess?" Yes, it was true, that was the one place that looked like we had lived here forever. I mean, where are you supposed to put things like dog toys and lightbulbs and batteries? Every other closet and drawer had its designated objects. Plus, we certainly hadn't had time to travel to Home Depot to buy stacking shelves, so we'd just shoved everything in there to prepare for the party.

"Here, Mimi," I said, opening the laundry room. I promptly pulled the vacuum out of the corner, handing it to my grandmother. It was the vacuum Mom had purchased at the hardware store on Madison Avenue, just two blocks away from our apartment. I wondered how we were ever going to get replacement parts.

"Jules, will you help Mimi vacuum?" Mom asked with an exasperated tone. She was now at the counter pouring beans into a large pot on the stove top. My mouth began to water—I loved barbecue beans.

"Uh, yeah, sure," I answered. Though I was a little unsure how you help someone vacuum when there is only one vacuum in the entire house.

Grandpa had turned on the TV and was watching the Rangers game. I glanced up and saw the Rangers led 2–0. *Score!*

"Jules, get up all this dog hair so it doesn't fill your vacuum," Mimi said. Her tone of voice was no longer happy-go-merry.

"Sure!" I said, trying to sound cheery. I pulled out a broom and began to sweep. "Okay," I said after about five minutes, "what now, Mimi?" Mimi couldn't hear me, as she was intently vacuuming the corner of our living room. Turning to dump the sweeping pan's contents into the trash, I saw Mom's urgent glance out of the corner of my eye. I spun around, wondering what in the world was wrong now. Mom was looking over to Mimi with her eyes opened wider than the Texas sky. *Another dust bunny?* Instead, I saw Creampuff—dear, dear Creampuff—pooping on the floor right behind Mimi, perilously close to her foot.

Why on earth did Creampuff choose that exact spot to take a dump? I thought, running to the bathroom. *I mean, really! Why not the cushy rug on the bathroom floor?* I quickly yanked on the toilet paper roll, sending the long line of soft white tissue swirling all over the floor. *I'll deal with that later,* I decided, skidding around the corner on my way back to the living room, almost running into our crystal cabinet. Thankfully, Mimi had her back turned and didn't see me gingerly pick up the moist dropping, hold it with my arm extended to its farthest capacity, grab at my nose, and run back to the bathroom to flush the whole wad down the toilet.

"Oh, there's Creampuff. Quick! Get her wee-wee mat!" Mimi said, her voice filled with angst.

"Don't worry. I got it handled," I said. "What are you doing, Mimi?" I asked as I watched her pick up the vacuum spout and begin waving it in the air around the couch and Grandpa.

"Lorraine, what are you doing? You're blocking the Rangers game," Grandpa muttered between a mouthful of Diet Coke, swatting the air.

"I'm about to vacuum the couch! But you know, a new study just came out in *USA Today* that said when vacuuming, 70 percent of the dust and dog hair flies into the air," Mimi said with an emphasis of disgust on her most despised words, *dog hair.* "See, see—there is a huge clump just floating above Maurice's head!" Mimi said as she twirled the vacuum nozzle and swiped it over Grandpa's head. The little piece of dog hair vanished into the dark abyss of the vacuum nozzle. Mom put a can of beans down on the counter and let her head fall into her hands.

"All right, Lorraine!" Grandpa growled as he pushed the power button of the vacuum, which had just run into his big toe. "Don't you need to be doing something else right now, like stirring the beans or cutting the vegetables?"

"Emily, are you stirring those vegetables? Oh my goodness! I left the red-white-and-blue ice cream in the car! All because I had to vacuum. Oh!" Mimi said as she flopped down onto the couch, very dramatically, her arms tangled over her face.

"I'll go get it!" I said slowly, and quietly I tiptoed to the door.

"No, no, no. I'll get it!" Mimi said, springing up.

"No, it's okay, Mimi. I'll get it."

"No one asked you to vacuum, Mom," I heard Mom say as I picked up the vacuum cord on the way to the door so no one would trip.

"Mm-hm," Mimi replied. I fast-walked to the car, crossing my fingers and toes that the ice cream would at least look salvageable. When I opened the car door, it was like opening the door to an oven, heat blasting across my face. I found the ice chest full of ice cream, soft drinks, and watermelon. *Oy vey.* Plus there were still bags of . . . What was that? Fireworks!

"Yippee!" I said to myself. "We have fireworks!" I lugged the ice chest out of the car and it hit the gravel drive with a loud thump. The ice chest turned out to be more of a problem than I expected: puny wheels do not roll well on gravel rocks. I lugged and lugged and lugged— over one rock, and then another rock, making progress stone by stone. Right as I reached the gate, a huge green beetle flew into my hair, obviously thinking it was help-ing me.

"Ugh! You, fly away now . . . That's right, fly away . . . No! Not into the fireworks bag!" I told the beetle. It did not move. Not wanting to bring the beetle into the house, I left the bag on the driveway and resumed my arm work-out with the ice chest.

When I walked back into the house, I blessed the per-son who invented air-conditioning. In my mind, it tied with refrigeration, lightbulbs, and motor vehicles for the most wonderful invention in the history of time award.

"Where have you been this whole time?" Grandpa asked, looking at me from above the rim of his reading glasses, his phone in hand. I assumed he was checking the stock market.

"Oh, well, Mimi does not pack lightly," I said. Sparkle meowed from Mom's upstairs bedroom, batting on the door. I guessed he had watched my circus show from the window overlooking our driveway.

"Is the ice cream *totally* ruined?" Mimi asked, swing-ing her arms wildly in the air before letting them fall limply to her sides. Mom looked at me from her vegetable-chopping post at the counter and rolled her eyes. *Drama queen.*

"Nope, trust me, there is plenty of ice left," I said as I opened the lid. I had heard the ice sloshing around all the food as I heaved the chest over the many rocks.

"Tech Support?" Grandpa beckoned me. He nick-named me Tech Support since I was always the one who talked him through how to use his electronic devices.

"Yes, Grandpa?"

"How do I delete this app?"

I whizzed my fingers over his phone. "Here you go."

He looked up at me from the couch with a wide smile. "You never cease to amaze me," he said.

I leaned over and kissed the top of his balding head. "My, my, my, don't you smell good," I said, winking at Mom. She giggled. "Is that the new shampoo and body wash we mailed to you for Valentine's Day?" I asked, flipping over the back of the couch and landing on the pillows next to him.

"Yes, Mimi made me take a bath," he said while rolling his eyes. "And I had to go get my beard trimmed," he added with a hint of pride in his voice, though he would never admit it.

"His beard looked like a caveman's and he hadn't had a bath—" Mimi began.

"My beard looked fine."

"No, it did not!"

"Okay, good behavior for Jules's sake, children," Mom said, now unloading the soft drinks from the heavy ice chest. Our whole kitchen island was soon covered in Mimi's stuff.

"*I* wasn't doing anything," Mimi said, washing the watermelon.

"Anyway!" I said, clapping my hands together and rolling off the couch.

"Oh! The guests will be arriving soon!" Mimi exclaimed as she lay the watermelon down on the table, leaning down on it as if she were about to collapse. "Oh! We still have to sweep the porch and lay out the table-cloths and clean another ice chest and put goodie bags together and set all the lawn chairs out!" Mimi cried as she began to cut the watermelon in supersonic motion.

"No need to stress!" I said, running to the back door that led to the rear porch where we kept our old ice chest.

"Don't open the—" Mom yelled, but it was too late. I opened the door and all four dogs ran inside: General, Chubbs, Buster, then Jessie.

"*Ah!*" Mimi screamed. "I just got these pants back from the cleaners. Shoo, dogs, shoo."

"O-kay!" I said, grabbing Jessie and Buster by the collars, wondering what else could possibly happen in this day. "Out you go!" I said, walking them back outside. "General, where are you?" I asked as I walked around the corner into the hallway. I found him lying down in my freshly cleaned room. "No! Don't you see you just tracked mud all the way through the house?" I whispered to him, reaching to grab his collar. He fell over onto his side, asking me to rub his tummy. "I have no time for this! Can't you tell we are in a great state of panic, and I just made it twenty times worse?" He thumped his tail. "Okay, pat-pat-pat," I said as I rubbed his tummy. "Now, up!" I said. Giving up on my futile attempts, I opened the door to the pantry and picked up a dog treat. "Come on, little General, I know you want a treat." He sat up in slow motion. "Come and get it." I said, tossing it onto the floor. He stood up and walked toward it. I snatched it up right before he could get it and then teased him to the door.

"Phew!" I exclaimed as I closed the door with all the dogs back outside. "Now, what was I doing?" I asked myself.

"Oh! The floor is all dirty again. Ew!" Mimi said, scrunching up her nose.

"Right. Ice chest."

I walked to the back porch and found our blue-and-white ice chest. Dead June bugs filled the cup holders on the lid. *Fantastic.* I hated June bugs. Deciding the ice chest needed some cleaning, I turned on the water hose and began to clean when I heard someone yell, "Jules!"

Oh no, it can't be.

"Jules!" My friend Miranda ran over and nearly knocked me over in a hug.

The guests were arriving. *This is not good.*

"We overestimated on the time it would take to drive out here—we thought it would take three hours and it only took two and a half—so we got here early. Can we help with anything?" Miranda asked. I gulped. *Help with anything?*

I had invited all the people I knew in Texas, as I figured my New York friends wouldn't fly all the way here on such short notice. That means I invited a total of two people. First, I invited Miranda. Miranda and I had met at a ballet summer camp in New York, instantaneously becoming best friends. Thanks to modern-day technology, we had kept in touch, and when I told her I was moving to Texas, she was over the moon. Second, I invited my one and only male friend, Austin (years of attending an all-girls school greatly limited my interaction with the opposite gender). Thankfully, Miranda brought her older sister, Rainey, so we had an even number of kids to participate in the fun and games.

"Yeah, come on inside," I told Miranda. "We still have a lot to do."

As we walked inside together, I yelled, "Miranda's here!"

"Oh!" Mom and Mimi shouted instantaneously. Mimi looked like she had seen a ghost.

"Hi, Miranda! It's so good to see you," Mom said, hugging my friend.

"Emily! Oh, it's so good to see your face." Miranda's mom entered the house behind us, walking over to greet Mom.

"Well, we still have a lot to do to get ready!" Mimi chimed.

"I'll set up the tables!" I said.

"Oh, I'll help!" Miranda responded. Together, we walked outside and covered the folding tables in red-white-and-blue tablecloths. Rainey brought out Mimi's new Fourth of July platters, which sure did add a nice touch to everything. I was just about to walk back inside when I saw Austin walking into the yard.

"Austin! Over here!" I yelled. Finally locating me, he walked over.

"Hey, Jules," he said. "Am I late?"

"Not at all. Miranda and Rainey just got here early. We are still setting up!"

Before we reached the house, Mom and Mimi were on the way out with the uncooked hamburgers and hot dogs.

"Now where's the grill?" Mimi asked.

"Over here," Mom said, leading Mimi to a rather dilapidated-looking portable grill.

"Oh, Emily, we can't put the hamburgers on yet—we have to scrub the grill first. This is *so* dirty! Where is your scrubber? Oh, here it is . . . Now, we have to use these tongs for the hot dogs, and these for the hamburgers. And we have to use one set of tongs for the meat and one set for the buns so we don't contaminate anything. And remember, we have to cook the hamburgers thoroughly so that we kill all the E. coli," Mimi was saying. Mom looked over at me with wide eyes. "Now, let's put the buns on one side and the meats on the other. Oh! Don't touch the buns without washing your hands!"

"Thanks, Mom. I don't know how I ever cooked hamburgers without you," Mom said, patting Mimi on the shoulder. "I really can do all this, Mom. You shouldn't be out here in this heat."

"No, no! I am perfectly fine," Mimi quickly replied, pushing up the sleeves of her red-white-and-blue summer shirt. It truly puzzled me that she could manage to wear anything but a tank top on a 98-degree day. She was still wearing her antlers, which I think she had forgotten about long ago, and her hair was dripping with sweat. I felt bad for poor little Mimi, who, despite the heat, continued to move like the Energizer Bunny. She just kept going, and kept everyone else going.

While waiting for the food, Austin, Miranda, Rainey, and I decided to catch up on some current events.

"Well, nothing is really new for me," Austin said in a bored tone. "Except we now have a little Chihuahua named Boa."

"Aww!" Miranda exclaimed, clasping her hands together.

"That's exciting," I said, slapping him on the shoulder. "How was school last year?"

"Boring as ever, except we dissected a frog in science class. That's about it."

"Ugh. I am not looking forward to dissecting anything . . . even if it is dead," I said as I shook my head. I'd heard horror stories from my cousin Robert about how his friends had to dissect a pig in science.

"It was really cool," Austin said. He said it in a tone that meant that actually he was cool for doing it.

"Well, I had a rabbit named Fluff, but Rainey here just *had* to have a snake," Miranda began, changing the subject away from frog guts.

"You know the only reason your little rabbit got eaten was because somebody *had* to save the little mice, which were my snake's food, and they promptly ran away." Rainey jumped to her own defense.

"Your rabbit got eaten by a snake?" I yelped. "Why did you have a snake in the first place?" I asked Rainey.

"Well, she wanted an 'exotic pet,'" Miranda said sarcastically, making quotation marks with her fingers.

"What kind of snake was it?" Austin asked, now intrigued.

"I swear it was a boa constrictor," Miranda said, thumbing her nose at Rainey.

"Whoa! A boa constrictor? I thought you had to have a permit to own those," Austin said, looking puzzled.

"It was not a boa constrictor!" Rainey said.

"Anyway!" I said, trying to change the subject. "I'm very sorry about your bunny, Miranda."

"So, what's up with you?" Miranda asked, crossing her legs on the hammock.

"Well, Mom and I are taking care of the ranch full-time now, which means taking care of all the animals, morning and night . . . Did I tell you about one of our little baby longhorns that disappeared last week?"

"Oh no! Did you find it?" Miranda gasped, clasping her hands over her mouth.

"Well, let me tell the story. Mind you, this was about my sixth day on the ranch. One of the younger cows, named Yellow Rose, gave birth to a beautiful little heifer. Yellow Rose is really young—she still has little stubby horns coming from her head—so she really shouldn't have been bred yet, but the bull jumped the fence line and . . . ya know . . . we have baby longhorns now. The baby was a pewter Oreo who—"

"What is a pewter Oreo?" Austin asked.

"If a cow has black on their sides and white along their backbone and stomach, Mom calls it an 'Oreo.' This little heifer, though, had pewter coloring along her sides and white along her backbone and stomach. She is really pretty," I said.

"I never knew cows could be pewter," Austin said.

"Tell us what happened! How did you find her?" Miranda asked.

"Okay, well, it all happened like this," I began, resituating in the hammock so I could narrate the story easier. "Mom and I were cubing the cows—"

"Cubing the cows?" Austin asked.

"Cubes are a protein supplement for the cows. They're shaped like big pellets and come in fifty-pound sacks."

Austin nodded his head in understanding.

"Anyway, Mom and I were cubing the cows when we realized that Yellow Rose was with the herd, but her baby was missing. Mom decided we should drive around in our four-wheeler to look for the calf. I was really scared because Mom told me it is never a good sign when a calf is away from the herd for that long. The calf was only a few days old. We first drove to the North Forty to look. But there was no sign of the calf anywhere, so we drove to the other side of the property to another pasture, which Mom calls the West Forty. The cows spend a lot of time back there, but since there is no pond or water source, they can't stay back there for long. We didn't find the baby there either.

"When we finally gave up our search and returned to the barn, it was almost dusk. The cows were still by the barn and scrounging the ground for a last remaining cube. Mom and I counted them one more time to see if the baby had shown up—because sometimes the calves just hide in the forest out of view. But now Yellow Rose was missing too!

"Mom and I weren't sure what to do then. We remembered that Sammer, our neighbor, told us that his cows sometimes hide their young—somewhere safe like in a dense thicket—and then go back and find them a few hours later. We had ruled out this theory because Yellow Rose had not left the herd once all day. A calf isn't supposed to go all day without its mother's milk, so we figured either Yellow Rose forgot where she hid the poor thing on the three hundred acres or the little calf was gone for good.

"Mom, determined not to give up, drove us back to the North Forty. When we reached the pasture, Mom killed the engine and we listened for a second, seeing if we heard Yellow Rose in the woods. The sun was setting and we just sat there as the sun slowly disappeared behind the trees. Everything was eerily quiet.

"Then all of a sudden, I heard something approaching behind us. *Crunch. Crunch. Crunch.* And there was Yellow Rose with her nose to the ground, walking toward us. All by herself too! She had bravely walked across the three hundred acres alone to find her baby. When Yellow Rose saw us, she stopped, lifted her head, and looked at us for a while, trying to see if it was safe to continue on or not. Mom motioned to me to not move a muscle. After what felt like ages, Yellow Rose lowered her pink nose to the top of the grass and followed an invisible line until she disappeared. A few moments passed and then, suddenly, I saw the rest of the herd walking up behind us. Mom told me the herd had come to protect Yellow Rose and her baby. If one cow is isolated from the herd, coyotes are more likely to attack. But there they all came, dozens of large blobs moving up the rolling hills in the fading light. If I hadn't known they were longhorns, I would have been spooked.

"We drove to the very end of the pasture, and there was Yellow Rose with a pewter-colored blob standing beside her, swinging its tail. It looked like it was nursing, so we decided everything was all right."

"Aw, yay!" Miranda and Rainey said together.

"I thought it was going to have more action than that," Austin said. He then decided to act out his version of the ending of the story. "And then the coyotes came running into the pasture and the baby ran for its life. I ran out and whisked the baby from the coyotes and they pursued me for miles and miles until I was back at the house!"

"Very funny, Austin," I said. "I don't like the thought of coyotes being anywhere near my baby calves."

"Boys," Miranda said, rolling her eyes.

"Hey!" Austin said defensively.

"Lunch is ready!" Mom yelled. All four of our heads whipped around and my mouth immediately filled with saliva.

Miranda hopped off of the hammock and took off.

"My stomach is about to eat itself because I'm so hungry. Did you know that our stomach secretes acid to help digest our food?" Austin asked, thinking he had just said something profound—his mother is a doctor.

"Yes, actually, I did. But did you know that cows have four stomachs to help digest the food they eat, and because they eat so quickly, they have to re-chew their food? They call that 'chewing their cud,'" I said, not moving from my very comfortable position on the hammock.

"All I know is that I'm hungry and you are trying to show off all the new, cool things you know that I don't," Austin said, looking down at me and pushing me off the hammock.

"Hey, watch it!" I laughed, finally standing up.

"Come on! The food has been ready for two whole minutes now!" Rainey exclaimed as she ran over to the porch to grab a plate. "All the adults have their food already!" she added, shouting over her shoulder.

"Wait for me!" I said, racing to catch up with her. "Beat you there," I said as I winked at Austin, who was still sitting, bewildered at how everyone but him was off the hammock and in the food line. I laughed and ran on. He would catch up eventually.

After rushing through the line and heaping our plates full of baked beans, potato salad, and coleslaw, we skidded to a stop behind the barbecue grill where Mom and Mimi were quickly serving the hamburgers and hot dogs. Grandpa entered the line right behind me.

"How are the Rangers doing?" I asked him.

"Ahead by four."

"Hamburger or hot dog?" Mom asked as I reached the front of the line.

"Definitely a hot dog."

Mom laughed, placing a hot dog on my plate.

"There, Jules. Now go get some mustard and ketchup," Mimi said, patting me on the shoulder. "Oh, those darn flies! Watch your food, please. Another one of those dreaded, despicable insects almost landed on your hot dog." She swished her flag-design paper napkin over my red plastic plate, surprising me greatly. My eyes darted down to see a small black fly searching in vain for a landing strip on my hot dog. Upon seeing Mimi's napkin, the fly resorted to landing on a forgotten piece of bread beside the grill and contently began to eat.

"I think Jules is perfectly capable of swishing the fly off her plate herself," Grandpa said, receiving his hamburger and reaching for the mustard. He squeezed the mustard bottle with a bit too much power, sending a dewy drop of yellow mustard onto a white stripe on his flag T-shirt. "Oh darn," he added with a sound of resentment.

Mimi leaned over to help Grandpa remove the stain. "I have it, Lorraine!" Grandpa said, swatting the air with his napkin.

"Move along, boys and girls, people are waiting," Mom said, pushing Grandpa gently on the back.

"It's okay, Grandpa," I said, patting him on the shoulder.

Miranda and Rainey whirled by me, waving bags of chips in their hands, trying to beat me to the circle of lawn chairs where Austin was sitting.

"Hey, Jules. What are we doing after this?" Rainey asked, sitting down in a chair beside Austin.

"Yeah! Are we going to ride R2?" Miranda asked, clapping her hands.

"Are we going to throw torpedoes at the cows and then have them chase us through the ranch?" Austin asked.

"Well . . . ," I said, plopping down in my chair. "Austin, we aren't going to try to get ourselves killed by playing with the cows. It might sound fun, but it's really not."

"So what are we going to do?" Austin asked, looking confused.

"We are going to have fun," I said, taking a huge bite out of my hot dog.

"Well, that is a given around here," Miranda said as she wiped her mouth with the back of her hand. I laughed and closed my eyes.

Miranda and I held the blue rope that bound my left leg to her right leg.

"We can do this," Miranda whispered, looking ahead with great determination, reminding me of Annie from *Toy Story*. The first event of our Fourth of July party was the three-legged race.

"Oh yeah," I replied as I brushed a piece of hair out of my eyes. It was blistering hot outside and my hair had that strange, sticky feel that happens whenever every ounce of your skin begins to drip with sweat. *I wonder what my New York friends would think of this heat. They would probably wilt like everything else.*

I glanced over at Rainey and Austin, our one competitor. They were quarreling over who held the rope. Mom and

I couldn't figure out what you were supposed to use to tie legs together, so we'd just used our horses' lead ropes. They wouldn't stay tied together without being a "tripping hazard," so we had resigned to holding the tails of the knot. The lead rope was awfully tight around my jeans-covered legs. I hadn't attempted to wear shorts, despite the heat, since Mom always thought a snake was close by and my legs had to be covered. Miranda, on the other hand, was wearing fashionable white shorts with a slightly low-cut T-shirt that had a pink hue to it. Her hair was brushed back into a ponytail with a fluffy pink tie to secure it. I was slightly envious of her sense of fashion. My "I'm the Future President" tank top defied all laws of girls' fashion. *Oh well,* I thought. *It's a good thing cows and horses don't care what I look like.*

"No, I want to hold my side," I heard Austin shout as he pulled the rope from Rainey's hands. Rainey whipped her head around to me and threw out her arms in exasperation.

"Are you going to do anything about him?" Rainey asked, almost squealing, trying to suppress a scream.

"Are you ready, boys and girls?" Mom said a little too happily. "Or should I say, boy and girls."

"We're ready!" Miranda shouted, bending down and about to take off. I could tell she said it quickly so Rainey couldn't complain.

"Miranda," I said, "don't drag me around this whole arena, please. We have to work together, you know."

"Yeah, I know. Just try to keep up with me," she said, elbowing me. I rolled my eyes.

"Okay! So, ready . . . set . . . go!" Mom said, throwing her hand in the air. As Miranda and I lunged together, I couldn't help thinking our years of friendship were beneficial in a three-legged race. Miranda's mom was at the other end by the finish line that was marked by a huge mud clump and a rooted tumbleweed. (Yes, it was probably just a recalcitrant weed, but a "rooted tumbleweed" just sounded better.)

I lunged in perfect harmony with Miranda and we gained a considerable distance from Austin and Rainey, who were whispering insults about who was doing what wrong. They looked like a wheel that had been thrown off course by a boulder, swaying to and fro with no sort of pattern. All of a sudden I felt a tug on my leg; the knot in the rope connecting our legs had widened because Miranda hadn't picked up her foot. I tried to look back at her, but before I knew it she had fallen and taken me with her. I landed with a thud and a stray piece of rock pierced my side. *That hurt*, I thought as I cringed and rolled into a strange contorted circle. Before I realized it, I saw Austin and Rainey suddenly speeding up, quickly gaining ground. I looked at Miranda, who was sprawled out on the ground a little behind me. Surprisingly, Miranda winked at me, as if this was all some sort of ingenious plan of hers. I couldn't believe my eyes as I watched Miranda kick her leg out at the exact moment Rainey was passing. *Oh no. You have got to be kidding me. Nope, Miranda isn't kidding.* Rainey tumbled first, swinging Austin's leg from under him.

"Come on!" Miranda said as she hopped up and yanked my leg with her.

"Watch it!" I yelped as the knot tightened. My ankle was receiving some major wear and tear from Miranda.

"Quick!" Miranda screamed, pointing to Rainey, who was on her hands and knees. "Ready! Left foot, right foot, go!" she said as she lunged. Thankfully, I had tightened the knot so tightly that my foot just traveled with hers. We managed to hop over the finish line right before Austin had finished retying their lead rope.

"What?" Austin yelled, defeated.

"Yeah, if you had just left it as it was and didn't try to make it a 'square knot' . . ." Rainey had her hand on her hip and started rolling her eyes.

"Yay!" Miranda said, jumping up and down. "We did it, we did it!"

"Yay," I said, exhausted, pathetically jumping. It took me awhile to notice that all the parents were laughing and doubling over.

"What's so funny?" Miranda asked, tightening her ponytail.

"I think we need a redo," Mimi said, walking over.

"You can't trip your sister like that, dear," Miranda's mother said, still laughing.

"What was I supposed to do? Let her walk by like that?" Miranda said, acting totally innocent.

"Personally, my ankle is telling me that either we move on, or my prize will need to be a huge ice pack," I said.

"Let's do the potato sack race now," Mom said. "I'll go and get the sacks from the house."

"Yay!" I said.

"What are we using for the sacks?" Austin asked me.

"Mom and I drove to the corner store about twenty minutes away, and he had some genuine potato sacks that he had been storing feed in. He let us buy them for a few dollars!" I said. By this time, Mom was entering the arena carrying those four sacks.

"Y'all ready?" Mom asked, passing out the potato sacks to us. We hopped in and lined up behind the starting line.

"Y'all are all going down!" Austin exclaimed.

"I wouldn't be too confident about that if I were you," Miranda replied. I wasn't sure how good I would be at a potato sack race, so I kept quiet.

"On your marks, get set, go!" Mom yelled, swinging her hand into the air. We all began hopping for our lives to the finish line. I quickly became the slowest.

"This is a *lot* harder than it looks," I yelled. Miranda was first with Austin at her heels. Rainey was third and gaining speed.

"It's fun!" Miranda exclaimed. I sighed. I had the unfair disadvantage of wearing five-pound-per-shoe snake boots while everyone else wore tennis shoes.

"I win!" Austin yelled victoriously. I collapsed onto the ground. *Potato sack races are obviously not my thing.*

By this time, the sun was setting and we all received prizes for our efforts in the games. They consisted of little American flags and red-white-and-blue sunglasses that Mimi had bought at the 99¢ Only Store.

"Do y'all want to fix s'mores?" Mom called.

"Yeah!" all four of us yelled at once. We ran to the top of the hill above the area where the fire pit was located.

"Oh, poor Maggie and Rocky. It's okay!" Mom called to the two horses who were now running around in their pastures. "It's just us! I guess they think the ranch is about to burst into flames," Mom said, talking to me now. "Oh! We have to feed!"

"Can I come?" Miranda gasped, overhearing our conversation.

"I'll come too!" Austin and Rainey added simultaneously. The four of us darted over to the barn with Mom.

"All right, come in here first, everyone," Mom said, leading the way to the feed room. "Rocky gets two scoops of Equine Senior." She dumped two scoops into a red bucket and handed it to me. "Maggie gets a scoop of Equine Senior and a scoop of rolled oats." She handed the next red bucket to Austin. "And R2 gets half a scoop of rolled oats." The final bucket was handed to Miranda. "Now we go out here." Mom led us all out of the room.

Rocky nickered from his stall. "Yes, Rocky, you are fed first," Mom said. She opened the door to the trough, motioning me to deliver the feed. I tipped over the red bucket, sending the feed into the trough.

"Is R2 next?" Miranda asked.

"No, no. Maggie is next!" Mom said. Maggie whinnied in response, waiting at her stall door. When she saw us coming, she spun around and pranced to the other end of the stall to her trough, pinning her ears and raring. Maggie began eating the air above her trough as if her food was already there. Taking the bucket from Austin, Mom dumped the feed into the trough. Maggie nose-dived.

"Now R2," Miranda said happily.

After giving R2 her oats in her mini trough, Mom led us all to the hay stall.

"Jules, climb on up to the top and grab one flake of alfalfa for Rocky, one flake for Maggie, and a half flake for R2," Mom said.

I slowly scaled the hay bales, my snake boots repeatedly failing to gain traction. I still hadn't gained my "hay legs"—so to speak.

"I fink I haf hay in my mouf," I said, tossing the flakes down to Mom.

"You look like a spider," Austin said, commenting on my strange position on the hay bales.

"Thanks?" I replied.

"Hop on down, Jules," Mom said, walking out to deliver the hay. By the time I had descended, all the horses were fed.

"All right, everyone, race you back to the fire pit!" Miranda yelled. A thunder of pounding feet resonated through the barn floor.

"Hold up!" I called.

When we all arrived back at the fire pit, panting and holding our sides, Mimi was already preparing the s'mores.

Grateful for the sweets, we all gorged ourselves on burnt marshmallows, chocolate, and graham crackers, reclining in our foldout chairs.

"Do y'all want some fireworks now?" Mom asked, finally making it to the fire pit—she hadn't joined us in our marathon sprint from the barn, so it had taken her awhile to catch up. We all nodded fervently, our mouths still full of s'mores.

"Oh, wait!" Mom exclaimed. She pulled four pamphlets out of her back pocket. I began laughing at once. "We have to all read the Declaration of Independence while the fireworks go off! You four"—Mom motioned to Miranda, Rainey, Austin, and me—"can take turns reading it aloud. We have to be patriotic! For that is what the holiday is all about!"

"All right," Austin said. "I'll start."

We took turns reading as the brilliant fireworks display illuminated the night sky. When we finished, we all curled up in our chairs and lit our sparklers, waving them in the air. I looked at my friends' faces: Austin was slumped in a lawn chair, waving his sparkler around aimlessly, obviously exhausted; Miranda and Rainey were sitting on the grass, poking each other with their marshmallow roasting sticks. I smiled and looked up at Mom. "This has been really fun," I whispered.

"I'm glad, sweetheart," she said as she gave me a strong hug.

Mimi and Grandpa sat on the periphery of the fire pit, holding hands while sharing a piece of apple pie. A crumb fell on Grandpa's stomach and Mimi rushed to flick it off.

"I got it, Lorraine," Grandpa sighed.

"All right," Mimi said, pecking him on the cheek. *They sure are nice to each other when they don't think anyone is looking.*

"Whoa!" I heard Miranda scream as one last purple firework lit the sky.

"Hurray for the red, white, and blue!" Mom began to sing, striving to be patriotic in all ways.

"May it wave as our standard forever!" I sang back.

Everybody joined in harmony as the fireworks blasted like cannons, sending sparkling colors into the starry sky.

Four

Mom and I had just completed our morning chores—feeding the horses, cleaning the stalls, sweeping the floor—when I saw Clover, our most amiable cow, quickly walking toward the barn. Her beautiful, broad horns absorbed the rays of the ruthless mid-July sun.

"Hi, Clover girl!" Her hard hooves clinked on the concrete walk-up leading to the barn. "How are you today?" I asked, bending over, my hands pressed firmly on my knees, acting like I was talking to a docile dog. She looked at me, unamused.

I walked to the feed room, where Mom was cleaning mice droppings off the feed table. The fluorescent light rod on the wooden ceiling flickered sporadically over Mom's head. *We will have to deal with that later.*

"Mom, Clover is here," I said, eyeing a daddy longlegs crawling on the doorframe above me, praying it didn't fall on my head.

"I swear, these mice poop like there is no tomorrow. I didn't know those little rodents excreted so much! It's utterly insane," Mom said as she wiped a small, black dropping into a cleaning wipe in an irritable fashion.

"Mo-om." I waved my hand in front of her.

"Yes, Jules?" she said, obviously still annoyed at the mice.

"Clover is here."

"Oh! Clover? She'll eat out of our hand!"

"She'll what?" Having longhorn saliva all over my hand was not high on my to-do list.

Mom propped up a brown sack of Special W Cattle Cubes and put some in a bucket. The smell wafted past my nose—not necessarily a bad odor, but it wasn't exactly the smell of fresh-cut red roses. "All right, follow me," she said, taking the bucket in her hand as she walked out the door.

"Hi, Clover girl!" Mom exclaimed. "Okay, Jules, take a cube like this . . ." She pulled out a long cube and grasped the very tip of it with her fingertips. "And then hold it out for her to eat."

I let Mom go first. She extended the cube to Clover, who stretched out her neck. Clover sniffed the cube, her large nostrils flaring. But she didn't take the treat.

"Clover, what's wrong?" Mom asked. "That's so strange. She always takes a cube."

As I stared at Clover, I could have sworn I saw a wave of worry flash through her black eyes. *I seriously need more human-to-human interaction,* I thought.

"Wait . . . Where is her baby?" I asked. I knew, at that very moment, something was wrong with her newborn son.

Clover had given birth to a little boy a few weeks before: a beautiful bull with a solid-black head and large black spots on an otherwise white body. Mom said one of his black spots looked like a dancing poodle; I said it looked like an elephant's head. But elephant or poodle, it did not matter. Mom said this calf was special because Clover had never birthed a bull before—it had "sentimental value." Somehow, though, all of our cows had sentimental value.

"Jules, look at Clover's udder," Mom said, pointing. It resembled a balloon on the brink of bursting. "That means her baby didn't nurse this morning . . . or last night."

I looked back at Mom. "Something's wrong, isn't it?"

Clover pawed the ground and swung her horns.

"All right, Clover, lead us to your baby," Mom said. "All we have to do is follow her," she added, looking at me. Right on cue, Clover turned around and started heading for the arena. As we followed Clover up the gravel road, my mind rushed to worst-case scenarios: the calf had broken its leg; the calf had died somewhere due to dehydration; the calf had wandered into a neighbor's pasture and was lost forever; coyotes had found the calf and now all that was left was a skeleton . . .

We followed Clover all the way to the old, dry ravine that ran behind our barn and arena. I ran ahead to investigate, following an old cow trail weaving around gigantic trees and over boulders. Finally, I reached the ravine.

"Stand back!" Mom warned.

"Mom! Look!"

I stood at the edge of a three-story drop-off. From the bottom, a baby calf looked at me with big, saucer-shaped eyes. The soil had completely eroded around the banks, making the inclines unclimbable. It looked like a disaster zone.

"How in the world are we going to get down there?"

Mom ran to my side and gasped. Without pause, she grabbed her cell phone from the front pocket of her bright red button-up shirt, wiping the sweat off her palms before dialing the phone.

"Sammer, are you home?"

"Yes."

"Clover's baby boy is stuck in the bottom of this dry ravine."

"Dry ravine? What dry ravine?"

"The one behind the barn."

"Well, how'd he git in there?"

"I don't know."

"I'm on my way," Sammer replied, sounding like Superman.

Sammer was over in two shakes of a cow's tail. After parking his four-wheeler at the edge of the tree line, he strutted over to us, asking, "Where's this calf at?" He once again wore his blue overalls and alligator-skin cowboy boots.

I pointed down to the bottom of the ravine.

"Well, what made you decide to fall in there?" Sammer asked the calf. The calf moaned a small moo. Clover mooed back, standing precariously close to the edge of the cliff beside us, looking down at her baby. "Hold this," Sammer said, handing me his cowboy hat. I expected him to pull out a lasso like in *True Grit*.

Before I could ask what he was going to do, Sammer began scaling down the three-story-tall ravine, holding on to the gnarled tree roots and rocks for support. His boots hit the bottom with a thud, sending up a cloud of dust.

"Whoo-ee, it's hotter than Hades down here!" Sammer yelled up. The tiny, helpless baby calf stood beside him on wobbling legs.

"How do you think he got in there, Sammer?" Mom asked.

"Well, Emily, it's hard to tell. But he probably fell through that hole there and tumbled straight down,"

Sammer answered, pointing up to the right at a hole in the deteriorating soil, covered slightly by the complex root systems that stretched across the ravine. "No saying how long he's been down here. He looks mighty dehydrated.

"Hey, Jules," Sammer shouted as he picked up the baby calf with his right hand, the muscles in his arm bulging as he bounced the calf onto the side of his hip. "Swing down that vine there. Should be strong enough for me to use." I wondered if my eardrums were beginning to wilt in this extreme heat. *A vine? His heroic plan is based on a puny tree vine?*

Nonetheless, I yanked on a young, thin, green vine looped around an old oak tree. My eyes followed the long, skinny stalk and found that it was rooted firmly beside the tree. I hoped for the best.

Sammer swatted at the vine and caught it in midair above his head. He twisted the vine around his right hand twice, seemingly indifferent to the fact the thorns would pierce his skin. The scene reminded me of Tarzan preparing to swing Jane around the forest—except here, Jane was a dehydrated baby longhorn.

"All right, here I come!" Sammer cried. He heaved up with one pull of his arm, and his entire face became bright red. *This is never going to work. This is simply never going to work.* The vine grew taut under the extreme pressure. Sammer slammed his foot in between two large, exposed tree roots that poked out of the ravine walls, sending a waterfall of dislodged dust and small pebbles down to the creek floor below. One of the dry, deteriorating tree roots, however, snapped, sending Sammer sliding back down to the creek bed. Not to mention his handy-dandy little vine snapped too. He stumbled back, slamming onto the dry riverbed, nearly crushing the little calf, whose black face seemed to be all screwed up and confused.

"Well." Sammer was at an apparent loss, and drenched in sweat. "I really thought that would work." I was about to walk a little closer to get a better look when Mom stuck her arm out to prevent me from tumbling over the cliff too.

"I guess we can use the rope I have in my four-wheeler," Sammer concluded. I wondered why he didn't use that in the first place.

Mom walked over to his four-wheeler and returned moments later with a long, coiled rope. After tying it securely to a large oak tree near the edge of the bank, she swung it down to Sammer.

"Is it secure enough, Emily?"

"I think so," Mom answered.

Sammer swung the baby calf over his shoulder like a sack of grain. It grunted, its little tail flopping around between its legs. "Okay, here we go." Sammer wrapped the rope around his wrist and then pulled with one arm, swinging his leg to the nearest foothold.

It worked. I couldn't believe my eyes; Sammer was scaling up an immense vertical incline with one arm and holding on to the calf with the other arm. Sammer's face turned a frightening shade of red, his lips pursed in determination.

Upon reaching the top of the embankment, Sammer tossed the calf over the ridge. It slid to a stop right at my feet with a little thump, his gangly legs all twisted into a complete mess. He just sat there on his back for a moment before he struggled to his feet, his coat caked in creek mud, his nose covered in spots of dirt. He sneezed.

Meanwhile, Sammer frantically grasped at the rope, struggling to climb over the edge. Clasping his arms around a thin tree trunk on the edge of the cliff, he heaved himself over to the top. He looked like a spider that had just climbed the Empire State Building.

"Phew! I ain't doin' that ever again!" Sammer said, wiping his hands on his overalls as he stood up. Mom nodded in agreement, relieved the whole dilemma was over now. Before I could say anything on the matter, Clover let out a moo like I had never heard before. It wasn't a hungry moo, it wasn't a "let us out of this pasture" moo, it wasn't a distressed moo . . . it was a mama's moo. The calf turned his head and let out a tiny, weak moo in return. It sounded more like a burp to me, but I could tell he was saying, "Mommy, Mommy, Mommy." Clover embraced her son with a long lick on his head, shaping his hair into an Elvis-style hairdo.

"Sammer," Mom started, "to show our immense gratitude, we are going to name this little bull after you. We'll call it P.S., for Paul Sammer."

Sammer was quiet for a moment. "Well, ain't that . . . nice." I don't think he fully appreciated the great honor of having a baby cow named after him—but he did seem to stand up straighter after Mom said it. I handed him his hat and he placed it on his head with pride.

"Jules, do you know the time?" Sammer asked, wiping his brow with his handkerchief.

"Um, let's see . . . It's eleven thirty."

"Eleven thirty? Oh, gracious me! I'm suppos'd to be at the railroad by noon! Well, as I like to say, all's well it ends well," Sammer said, walking over to his four-wheeler.

"Thanks, Sammer! I really do appreciate this," Mom said. "See y'all later!"

"That was exhausting," I sighed.

"But thank goodness Clover's baby is okay. Little P.S.," Mom said, watching P.S.'s tail spin around while he sucked on his mother's milk with little streams of milk oozing out the side of his mouth and onto the forest floor. Clover looked over at us. I could swear she said, "Thank you." I nodded my head at her. *I was happy to help.*

Before little P.S. was finished nursing, Clover walked to join the rest of the herd that was napping in the distance. "She's so proud of her baby boy," Mom sighed.

"How about we go to the house for some lunch?" she asked. I nodded vigorously. It sounded like a great idea.

We walked back through the forest, following the cow trail. Suddenly, the trail split.

"Which way do we go?" Mom asked me. I had no idea.

"Um . . ." I looked left and right. "The one on the right looks newer, so let's take that one."

"I'm not so sure."

"Come on, I'm almost positive."

We trudged forward in silence for a while, stepping carefully over bushes and ducking under hundreds of low-lying branches. The longhorns had the advantage of, well, long horns that could move all the debris out of the way. All I had was my head and hands.

"Everything is so dry!" Mom said, commenting on the wilting leaves on the trees. The whole world looked like it could use a torrential downpour. "We really need rain. Sammer said we've been in drought conditions for ten years now. He thinks it's a record."

"I think my sweat would be a great rain-replacer," I said, wiping some from the back of my neck and then flicking it off of my sopping hand. "I certainly have enough of it."

"Whoa, what's that?" Mom asked, stopping in her tracks. She pointed ahead to something in the trail. Mom pushed her glasses farther up her nose.

"It looks like a bird," I said.

"Why is it so strangely shaped, though?"

We walked closer, tiptoeing on the crackling leaves, trying not to disturb the bird. It let out an eerie alarm cry as we approached.

"It looks injured," I said. The bird lay in the middle of the path, favoring its one wing. It moved its hurt wing back and forth, as if indicating that it was broken. I scowled. I hated seeing wounded animals. "Do you think there is anything we can do?"

Mom was silent for a moment. "Well, we could try to see if it will let us take it up to the house."

"You mean, pick up the bird and take it to the house?" I asked.

"Otherwise it is just going to get eaten out here. It's so pretty—look at its black-striped neck, brown head, and white underbelly. It looks like it was painted!"

The bird called out again, still not moving from its position on the trail. Something rustled in the forest beside us. I assumed it was a fellow bird.

We slowly crept closer, until we stood about ten feet from the bird. Its large black eyes looked so frightened.

"All right, I'll pick it up, Jules. Do not, I repeat, do not touch the bird."

I nodded. Mom walked forward. Just as she reached down to pick it up, the bird flew up, screeching frantically. Mom flew backward, falling right on top of me. We landed in a pile on the trail.

"What in the world?" I asked. "Obviously, it wasn't wounded."

Mom scrambled to her feet, readjusting her glasses. "Oh, you know what? I remember now."

"Remember what?"

"That bird is called a killdeer. The male will act like it is wounded to distract predators away from the nest."

"Does that mean there's a predator around its nest?" I asked.

"Eh, we might have walked by it."

"How do you know all that?"

"I love birds." It was true. Mom was obsessed with birds, often reading the National Audubon bird guides in her free time. "Now, let's get back to the house for some lunch."

We continued walking along the trail, and eventually I could see a gravel road beyond the trees. "Finally!" I sighed. We emerged out onto the gravel drive and into the full wrath of the sun. Just as I began walking toward the house, however, something whizzed by me, throwing me completely off balance. "Yikes!" I yelled, falling back into the grasses.

"What in the world?" Mom exclaimed. "R2?"

"You have got to be kidding me," I mumbled. I looked to my left and saw a brown blob running through the open field, its tail straight out behind it like a wind sock. *I guess that's where the saying "high-tailed it out of here" comes from.* A piercing whinny came from the brown blob. It looked like R2, but who could tell? It actually looked more like the Tasmanian Devil from the Looney Tunes cartoon—her legs were running so fast they seemed to be turning in circles underneath her.

"Rocky?" Mom wailed. I looked to my right and saw Rocky, also running free, making his way toward us. I scrambled to my feet to avoid getting trampled.

Rocky quickly pranced toward us with his old movie-star grace, his black hooves clopping against the gravel road. His shiny black coat and long, bouncing tail gave him the appearance of a winged Pegasus—minus the wings. He pranced right by us, looking at us from his twinkling eyes as if asking, "Can you see me? Look at me, I'm free!" But all the while, he looked very uncertain as to where he was going, his ears rotating back and forth. He obviously knew he was breaking the rules, glancing over at Mom with that look of a young boy caught with his hand in the cookie jar. Once he passed us, he attempted a little buck, but due to his old arthritic knees, it looked like a stiff-legged jump in the air. I figured he was trying to imitate one of the wild Roman horses from the Trojan War. He arched his neck gallantly, thrusting his legs in front of him, imagining his old glory days.

"How on earth did he get out? Rocky is too old to be running around! He is going to hurt himself. Oh, for Pete's sake!" Mom exclaimed.

"Who's Pete?" I asked. Before Mom could answer, R2 once again whizzed past us, sending a strong current of wind across my face. One moment she was in front of me, the next she was a mile down the road, leaving nothing but gravel dust in her wake. *Who knew R2 could run that quickly?*

"Come on, Jules!" Mom exclaimed, running after Rocky, who was moving considerably quickly despite his age. "Who knows where they might go!" As I had discovered with Maggie on my first day on the ranch, the problem with a three-hundred-acre ranch is that if a horse manages to escape, there is no way to control where they go or when you can find them. When two horses escape . . . well, that's even worse.

Mom coughed twice and felt her pulse on her neck. "I think I'm in a-fib," she said, coughing twice again. Before I could say anything, however, she instructed, "Go get their halters." She ran toward Rocky, calling his name and demanding he stop, and I peeled the other way, running as fast as I could to the little blue barn at the foot of the hill.

"Just . . . keep . . . moving," I gasped. Halfway to the barn, I had to stop and double over to catch my breath. My snake boots once again felt like ten-pound weights on either leg. Finally, I gathered up enough strength to jog pathetically the rest of the way, flailing my arms to try to gain momentum.

Maggie greeted me with a nicker upon my entrance. Too winded to respond, I skidded through the barn and found Rocky's stall as open as the Texas sky; R2's stall door was open as well.

"I guess I forgot to latch their stalls, eh, Maggie?" I asked, frantically unhooking the halters and lead ropes from the barn wall. "Could you please tell them in horsey language to come back so Mom and I don't have to chase them around this entire ranch like two chickens with our heads cut off?" I gasped through my labored breathing, taking off once again through the barn. She snorted and shook her head. I had a feeling she was in cahoots with the others.

"That took a long time. What happened?" Mom asked when I finally caught up with her.

"It's kind of hot," I replied, catching my breath after yet another long run. My head felt considerably lighter than it should have. Rocky stood about twenty feet away from us, idling in the shade of the large oak tree. His head was to the ground, his mouth nibbling on blades of thin green grass. I was amazed there was any green grass left. I hadn't seen a single raindrop since we had moved to the ranch.

"Where's R2?" I asked.

"She dashed right by me again while you were at the barn. She's probably somewhere between here and the front gate right now," Mom replied. "I didn't know that pony could move so fast."

"I bet she's having the time of her life," I replied, peering through the hot air in hopes of catching a glimpse of my speed-demon pony.

"Come here, Rocky," Mom began coaxing, slowly approaching her horse. Rocky immediately popped up his head, seemingly ambivalent as to whether he should run or let Mom catch him. Before he could decide, however, R2 came barreling back from the front gate. She whinnied so long and loud it was as if she was yelling, *"Whee!"* as she ran toward us, her tail parallel to the ground. She looked like a young girl experiencing her first roller coaster: overcome with the thrill of it all. She came to a screeching halt behind Rocky, as if attempting to hide behind him so we wouldn't catch her. Dust floated in the air, enveloping both horses in a hot, dusty haze. Rocky, now very confused, spun around in a circle to look at the very energetic R2. She was still nickering and panting. He snorted and swung his head in the air. Out of exasperation, he then turned and began walking toward Mom.

"Good boy, Rocky! Come on, that's a good boy, come on," Mom said. "Got ya!" Mom swung the halter around Rocky's face. Upon seeing Rocky's capture, R2 attempted to run again, but I caught a handful of her mane just as she began to sprint away.

"R2, stop!" I yelled as she began to drag me through the grass. I yanked down on her mane and finally succeeded in slowing her to a halt. Before she could decide to take off again, I latched the halter around her face. R2's ears drooped slightly and her energy level instantly decreased by about 50 percent.

"Now, you two, we are going back to the barn," Mom said. "What were you *thinking* running around like this, Rocky? You are too old to be doing such things," Mom told Rocky as if she were talking to her son. Rocky looked over Mom's shoulder and gave me a very uncertain look.

"Heaven forbid I actually *ride* you back to the barn, R2," I told my pony. I hadn't attempted to mount her since she had decided to take a nap in the middle of our trail ride. I wasn't about to try it again until the weather cooled. R2 definitely did not mind.

After what felt like a journey across the Mojave Desert, we made it back to the barn, all sweaty and exhausted. Maggie whinnied, feeling very left out of the whole experience. "I know, Maggie," Mom said. "Can you believe they ran off like that?" Maggie stood in her stall in front of her little box fan. Her nose almost touched the fan, her long forelock and mane blowing backward as if she were posing for a magazine cover . . . or maybe a Pantene shampoo commercial. All she needed was her photographer.

After putting Rocky and R2 in their stalls—and making sure their doors were latched this time—Mom collapsed into the rocking chair. "Now I really need lunch," Mom groaned.

An hour and a half after food was originally suggested, Mom and I finally reached the porch.

"As long as I live . . . I will never be hungry again," I muttered, quoting Scarlett O'Hara from *Gone with the Wind* before collapsing onto the porch floor. Thinking I came bearing food, all four dogs came swarming toward me. General came first, nosing my elbow before flopping down on his back beside me. Buster came next, accidentally stepping on my hair. "Ow! Buster, come on, dude," I sighed. "General, Buster . . . No, Jessie, don't step on my face . . . Ew, your breath smells like horse manure . . . Now your saliva is in my eye, Buster . . . No, Jessie, don't scratch my face . . . Come on, Chubbs, really?" Chubbs carried her metal dog food bowl, hoping I would fill it with food. She promptly dropped it next to my head, nearly bursting my eardrum. All four dogs swarmed over me, licking my arms and face and making it impossible to sit up. I slowly began to feel suffocated by hot doggy breath. *What would life be like without dogs?* I thought. *Dull.*

After lunch, I fell face-first into the couch.

"Are you okay?" Mom asked, still sitting at the table.

"I'm resting," I replied, my voice muffled by a fluffy pillow that smelled strongly of Chubbs. Upon sitting up, I found that, in fact, it was Chubbs, who had decided to take a nap on the couch as well.

"Why don't you read a book or something?" Mom asked, always yearning to enrich my literary knowledge. I stumbled over to the bookshelf, leaving Chubbs to daydream on the couch by herself. Tilting my head, I scanned the titles: *Texas: A History*; *The History of Morningside County*; *The Chisholm Trail*; *The Red River: A Photographic History*; *Anson Jones: A Life*; *Gene Autry: A Biography* . . . I stopped. Gene Autry sounded interesting. After pulling out the book and brushing off the dust, I sat on the window seat. Creampuff hopped up and sat in my lap.

"What did you pick?"

"*Gene Autry: A Biography.*"

"Oh, Gene Autry? He was the famous country-western singer who lived around here. He sang that song I taught you when you were little, 'Deep in the Heart of Texas.' Don't you remember it?"

I gave Mom a puzzled look. I didn't remember.

I remained in the house for a while, reading about Gene Autry's childhood and Texas in the first decade of the 1900s. After a while, however, I found myself gazing out at nature. I felt like a fish in an aquarium: everything interesting was happening on the other side of the glass. I concluded that in order to concentrate, I should take after Christopher Robin and sit under a tree to read my book. I put Creampuff down on the floor and stood up. She promptly ran over to Mom and jumped into her lap. *So much for loyalty.*

"I'll be back, Mom!" I said. "I'm going to go sit in Maggie's pasture."

"All right, I'll be down in a little bit. It's almost time to feed the horses," Mom said, sitting at the table writing something in her journal—probably poetry.

A nice breeze had picked up, freshening the warm air. With my book tucked under my arm, I forged my way through the knee-high grasses in Maggie's pasture, grasshoppers fleeing in front of me like ocean spray. Stopping at the first shady spot in the pasture, I sat down under a large oak tree. I decided not to inspect the ground for bugs. *Ignorance is bliss.* A cool breeze rustled through the trees and the sun peeked through the canopy of leaves, designing the floor with kaleidoscopic patterns.

I had barely finished the first page when I felt something rustle my hair.

"Maggie!" I exclaimed, seeing a horse's nose an inch above my head. Her large brown eyes looked down at me. From my perspective, I could clearly see the white spot that covered half of her nose. I was amazed to see that the spot lined up perfectly between her top lip and bottom lip, as if she had dipped the side of her mouth into a bucket of white paint before she was born. "I thought you were in the barn," I told her. She bent her head down, pressing her nose lovingly into my chest, her warm breath rolling over my skin. Her breath smelled like freshly cut grass and carrots. I tickled the tip of her nose with my hand—it was so soft, like the fur of a baby bunny.

I stood up and wrapped my arms around her, her long mane falling over my face. It was every color of the sandy beaches: white, gold, blonde, beige, even some dark brown. "How are you doing today, Maggie?"

She tossed her head.

"Okay, okay, I won't hug too tightly," I said, releasing my grip. She pressed her nose into my side again, closing her eyes, her long eyelashes trembling. Suddenly, she took off, trotting in a little circle. The setting sunlight played in her tail, illuminating each individual strand of her thick tail, which trailed over the high grasses. She skidded to a halt in front of me, snorting and tossing her mane, her light brown hooves sending up a cloud of dust.

I laughed. "What are you doing? Do you want to play?"

She trotted in another tight circle, nickering with every stride. She walked up to me and pressed her nose to my side.

"All right, all right," I said. I mimicked her by turning in a circle and then skidding to a halt in front of her with my arms wide open.

She turned around and then tossed her mane.

"I'm gonna get you!" I called, running toward her. She took off, looking back at me. I sprinted after her, barely able to keep up. Suddenly, she stopped, causing me to dash past her.

She tossed her mane and whinnied her deep-throated whinny, thinking she had won.

"You little rascal," I teased, stopping to catch my breath. The sunlight shimmered on her coat, giving the illusion that she herself was radiating light.

I jumped toward her. She pranced around in a little circle.

I darted to the side. She darted in front of me.

"Hmm. I see what you are doing here."

I took off running away from her.

She zoomed past me.

"Hold up! I can't go that . . . Whoa!" I tripped on a gigantic weed and fell on my hands and knees. I rolled to my back, laughing. "Maggie, you're wearing me out!" I shouted to the air.

I just lay there looking up at the sky, watching the clouds move by. Suddenly, Maggie's head obstructed my view. Her breath blew across my face, once again filling my nostrils with scents of grass and carrots. She nickered, nudging my side.

"I'm not getting up. I'm exhausted. In one day alone, I have rescued a baby longhorn, endured an attack by a random killdeer bird, and chased Rocky and R2 around the ranch. Does that sound normal to you?"

She shook her mane.

"Right. I agree."

She nudged me again, trying to roll me over.

"Okay, okay, fine."

I stood up and stroked Maggie on the neck.

"You're such a good girl, Maggie."

She craned her neck as if to hug me. Leaning my head on her strong shoulders, I closed my eyes. I stood there for a while, just embracing Maggie, letting her nuzzle my shoulder. For that moment, I felt as if nothing else existed in the world—just my Maggie and me, the pasture spreading out around us indefinitely. The sun began to brush the tops of the trees, painting the entire world around us with a golden hue.

But at a ranch, peace is always limited.

"Jules!" Mom called. "Time to feed!" She was already at the barn.

Maggie's attention snapped toward the barn as she realized, suddenly, that she was famished.

"Okay, let's get your food," I told her. "Beat you there!" We raced back together, running at full speed.

In New York City, loud nighttime noises were quite commonplace. Thus, while living there, I had grown accustomed to hearing people shouting below my window at all hours, the revving engine of some vehicle on the street at four in the morning, and the random thumps and crashes from the floor above me that often interrupted my dreams.

At a ranch, however, none of this is supposed to happen.

So when I heard loud footsteps outside my window at four in the morning and saw headlight beams illuminating my ceiling, I was completely paralyzed. Mom's bedroom was located right above mine, but in order to reach her room I had to run by a wall of uncurtained windows and up a staircase that just happened to be right in front of the door. I suddenly missed our small, four-room apartment. The house was completely quiet, except for Creampuff's sporadic snoring—she had once again fallen asleep on my pillow, pushing me to the bottom of the bed.

For one peaceful moment I thought that the footsteps vanished, that the whole thing was just an extended nightmare. *Maybe that bright light is just the moon,* I thought, looking at my illuminated ceiling.

But then something slammed into the back door.

Bang, bang, BANG! A strong fist pounded on the door.

That's it. I ran with all my might through the house, dodging around four sleeping dogs. *So much for watchdogs.* Flying up the stairs, I burst into Mom's room, slamming the door behind me. Upon hearing my entrance, she sat up straight in bed, her blonde hair sticking out every which way. She screamed.

Not knowing why she was screaming, I screamed at the top of my lungs.

Mom screamed again.

I screamed.

Mom screamed.

I dived into Mom's bed, still screaming, skidding underneath a mountain of pillows and disturbing Sparkle, who proceeded to whop me in the nose with his paw.

"There's someone at the door. There's someone at the door," I repeated in a strong whisper. Sparkle suddenly growled from the pillow above me like he was a watchdog. *He's been around canines for too long.*

"Where are my glasses? Where are my glasses?" Mom asked, her tone of voice high and shaky. I groped around in the pitch black, running my hands over the entire king-sized bed to try to find Mom's glasses. Finally, my hand hit the metal rims and I shoved them into Mom's hand before burying myself once again under the pillows.

The back door trembled once more. The mysterious person knocked with all his might: *BANG, BANG, BANG.*

"Get up!" Mom yanked me into the bathroom, not waiting for me to in fact get up, leading us to our safety spot. Everything around me was veiled in darkness, but I wasn't about to turn on the light. Mom quietly closed the bathroom door and locked it.

"What about the pets?" I asked Mom.

"They will be okay."

I wondered how she knew that.

She started stepping into a pair of navy sweatpants and pulled on a sweatshirt over her gray, knee-length flannel nightgown. The sweatshirt read "Texans Don't Dial 911" and had a gun on the front.

Bang, bang, bang! The intruder had walked around to the front door. Mom immediately crouched down beside me. After a second, I heard his boots slowly crunch the dry grass as he walked around to the side of the house. I realized at that moment that if I were to scream for help, there was a high chance no one would hear me . . . ever.

"Hello!" a high-pitched male voice shouted.

I remained completely still, hardly daring to breathe.

"Hello!" the man shouted even louder.

"I need to get my gun," Mom said, crawling over to her closet. I could barely make out her silhouette in the darkness.

"Hello! Is anybody home?"

I don't remember the serial killer from Texas Chainsaw Massacre *ever announcing his arrival.*

Mom crawled out of the closet with her shotgun slung over her shoulder. "Should I answer back?" Mom asked.

"No! It could be a trap!" I whispered, pulling on Mom's gray nightgown so she would sit down beside me.

"Your longhorns are out on the road!" the man called.
No, not a trap.

"Who is opening all of our gates?" Mom yelled. She burst out through the bathroom door and ran to the window. "We're coming! One second!" Mom flew down the stairs.

I still sat paralyzed in the bathroom.

"Hurry up, Jules!" I bolted out of the bathroom and joined Mom. She was already in her boots, walking out the door—and had obviously forgotten about her outfit. I slid into my boots and ran after her. Since I hadn't had time to change, I still wore my bright orange Nike shorts and Tweety Bird pajama top.

"Sorry to waken you, ma'am," the man said as we walked down the porch steps, "but your cows are out on the main road, and at this time of night there's no sayin' who may drive right into them." He stood about five foot four, his voice was high and chipper, and his long gray beard shook back and forth as he talked. In the dim light coming from the moon, his light blue eyes twinkled from under his baseball cap. "My name's Mason Wilson, by the way." The man extended his hand to a very frazzled-looking Mom.

"Hi, Mason. I'm Emily O'Connor. Thank you so much for letting us know." Mom began walking through the yard to the driveway. Her sweatpants fell over the tops of her snake boots, which were on the wrong feet. As we walked onto the road and into brighter light, I could see her blonde hair sticking out from her head like a halo. "How did you get on the property?"

"Well, your gate is wide open! That's how the cows got out. I can help you round 'em up if you need. I was on my way to work, but it don't matter if I'm a bit late."

The three of us walked together down the driveway. Mason had a huge extended-size pickup truck with giant searchlights bolted to the roof. The bumper of the truck was covered in stickers: the symbol of the Deathly Hallows from Harry Potter, one proclaiming "I'm ready for the zombie apocalypse," a large American flag, then "I love the Constitution" and "Don't Mess with Texas." I liked Mason already.

Mom and I hopped on the four-wheeler and followed the man's truck down to the long gravel road to the gate. Exhaust filled the air. Since I sat in front of Mom on the four-wheeler, I received the brunt of the insect nightlife: bugs pelted my face and arms, a tiny moth flew up my nose, a June bug flew straight into my eye, and a large green leaf bug missed my open mouth by a millimeter. It's amazing how much I took windshields for granted.

When we got to the gate, we found it wide open and five of our longhorns grazing right outside it by the mailbox. *The grass is always greener on the other side.* Thankfully, the road was isolated. Mason pulled his pickup truck out onto the street and put his hazard lights on, blocking one lane so the longhorns wouldn't proceed any farther across. Dark road extended to the right, and more dark road extended to the left. I couldn't see anything for miles. One lone light shone above our gate, attracting hundreds of beetles that repeatedly slammed into the bulb.

Mom let out the loud cattle call Sammer had taught her. If our neighbors had been close enough, she would have awakened every last one of them.

"Whe-e-e-e-w!" she yelled. Her voice echoed through the still night. All five longhorns immediately lifted their heads. Four came running through the gate, fully expecting cubes, but one of them stood behind the fence, wondering how in the world to get to the other side. I could barely make out the cow's face in the darkness. "Come through the gate, goofus!" Mom said. The longhorn obviously didn't see that the gate was one hundred feet to its left.

"Who is that?" Mom asked me, pointing to the cow.

I wasn't sure, although it looked a lot like Revolution.

"Oh, it's Liberty!" Mom said. "Revolution's daughter should be smart enough to figure out how to walk through a gate."

"I got 'er!" the man yelled, jumping from his pickup truck, which was unnecessarily high off the ground. He walked behind Liberty and began motioning her forward with his arms. "Come on, girl. Come on."

Liberty looked very concerned and quite perturbed that her early-morning snack was interrupted. Thinking she was being led into a trap, Liberty took a sharp turn and ran into the road.

"No, no, no, come back!" Mom yelled, sliding off the four-wheeler to help Mason wrangle Liberty through the gate. Liberty looked very confused, running in circles and darting all about. Mom moved around Liberty like a basketball player on defense, her arms wide open and her feet pivoting every which direction—although her long nightgown significantly inhibited her range of motion. Finally, Mom managed to get behind Liberty and ushered her through the gate as Mason jogged alongside to prevent the escapee from darting back into the road. Before Liberty and the other four cows could realize that we did not, in fact, have cubes for them, I jumped off the four-wheeler and closed the gate, making sure to latch it with the lock.

"Phew!" Mom sighed, leaning against the gatepost.

Suddenly, a tractor emerged from the darkness and rolled down the road. The huge wheels seemed even larger in the darkness, and its headlights beamed across the road like the searchlight in a lighthouse. The tractor seemed to slow down for a second upon seeing Mason's pickup truck in the middle of the street. But it kept moving, once again disappearing into the darkness. *Grandpa always told me that real cowgirls get up with the sun, but the sun isn't even up yet.* All these people who were already awake just had to be nocturnal.

"Once again, sorry to bother y'all," Mason said once the roar of the tractor vanished.

"Don't apologize. Thank you so much for taking the trouble to help us," Mom said, tucking her blue sweatpants into her backward boots again. Her sweatshirt had fallen off one shoulder. "You live around here?"

"I live about ten miles north. Not a big place, but I have the nicest yard in the area," Mason bragged.

I didn't know real yards existed around here.

"What's your name, little missy?"

I hadn't talked the whole time. I wasn't even sure my vocal cords were working or if they were still paralyzed from fright. "Jules," I croaked.

"Nice to meet you, Jules. Well, I better be off. Have to go put up some fencin' over in the next county. Tryin' to get an early start before this blasted heat gets too bad. Nothing like July in Texas! See y'all around!" He tipped his hat and waved before roaring off into the distance. I watched his taillights slowly grow smaller down the dark road until they completely disappeared.

"We'd better go find the rest of the cows and make sure only these five escaped through the gate," Mom said. I wondered how we would be able to see the longhorns in the pitch dark. As we drove back up the gravel road, the five rebellious longhorns followed our lead, still hoping to receive cubes. The rest of the herd was nowhere to be found—at least nowhere within the range of our four-wheeler's headlights. Right as we approached the house, however, the headlights revealed a herd of sleeping cows. Miraculously, they were all present and accounted for.

"Well, at least we won't have to call the sheriff's office and report a missing cow," Mom joked. I giggled, stifling a yawn.

"Mom, what in the world is that?" I pointed to an ostrich-like animal that had made its way to the front of the four-wheeler. I wondered if I was now hallucinating, or if this whole event was a crazy dream.

"I didn't think ostriches existed here."

I suddenly felt like I had entered a scene from *Out of Africa*.

"Are you sure it's an ostrich?" I asked.

"I have no idea." Mom inched the four-wheeler closer to the animal. "You know what, Jules, I think it's an emu . . ."

"A what?"

"An emu . . . Except they are only supposed to live in Australia."

Before we could say anything more, the emu walked into the tree line and disappeared.

"We're going back to bed before anything else happens," Mom said. That sounded like a great plan to me.

Five

'Mayday! Mayday! We are under attack. We have found three nuclear missiles off the coast of Virginia!'

"'Do not fire back. I repeat, do not fire back,' General Johnson said.

"'But, sir, we are under attack. I am now seeing three nuclear missiles about to launch onto the mainland. If we fire now . . . ,' Captain Kurtt said urgently.

"'Do not fire!'"

It had been Mom's idea to read this book about the end of the world. I really don't know why she wanted to read it, but she did. Much to my surprise, it was an interesting read. As part of my literary education, Mom insisted that we read a book aloud together every summer—we had started when I was five.

So there we sat on the front porch, surrounded by the humming of hundreds of flies, reading this book out loud in the heat of a mid-August afternoon. I swung back and forth on the wooden porch swing while munching on half of a turkey and cheese sandwich. At my feet, Chubbs looked up at my sandwich with saliva dripping from her pink tongue. "This is mine," I told her. She closed her mouth and tilted her head, her tail waving back and forth like a propeller engine. "Oh, don't give me the puppy-dog eyes. This is my sandwich." She sat down, not removing her eyes from my food. "Okay, fine," I sighed, tearing off the crust. Chubbs inhaled it before it even touched the ground.

At the sight of food, the three other dogs swarmed over to me, expecting a treat. "No, this is my midafternoon snack and I am going to eat it myself," I said, holding my plate over my head and out of range of the four dog snouts now furiously sniffing around my chair. Before I could be guilt-tripped into donating my entire snack to the Hungry Spoiled Dog Fund, I saw something move out of the corner of my eye.

"Oh, look!" I said, right as Mom was about to continue reading. "The longhorns are walking up."

Sure enough, the whole herd slowly plodded their way up the gravel road, their horns swaying back and forth as they walked. They reminded me of the cattle that pulled covered wagons on the old pioneer trails, one following right after the other and never veering from their course.

"We might as well count to make sure they are all here," Mom said, standing up and walking to the edge of the porch. As the long procession moved by the house, I counted in my head. Thankfully, all were present.

"Oh no, what is that little one doing?" Mom groaned, walking to the front steps of the porch. One of the baby longhorns had somehow managed to get inside the arena and was now trotting around, unsure of how to exit, obviously oblivious to the open gate at the far end.

I stood up next to Mom and we walked down the front porch steps to stand in the lawn. Jessie followed at my heels, staring up at me with a look of intelligent intensity.

"Do you think it will figure out how to get out of the arena on its own?" Mom asked.

"I'm not sure. How would we get it out, though?"

"We could walk over there and open the other gate." There were gates on either end of the arena, but the gate closest to the baby cow was latched shut.

Jessie still sat at my feet, following our gaze and watching the baby cow.

"Surely it's smart enough to go out the same gate it entered through," I suggested.

The baby calf mooed at the rest of the herd, who seemed ignorant of the whole situation.

Or maybe not.

"I guess we have to go open that other gate," Mom said. We walked to the end of the white picket fence around the house, Jessie still following me. I assumed she was still waiting for a piece of sandwich. Right as I swung open the fence gate, Mom stopped me, saying, "Wait, hold on." The baby cow had turned around and looked squarely at the open arena gate. But then it turned back toward the closed gate and let out another long moo.

"All right, let's go."

Just as Mom lifted her leg to walk out the picket fence gate, Jessie bolted by us, running through the gate, across the gravel road, through the pasture, and straight into the arena. The little longhorn spun around upon hearing Jessie slide through the pipe-and-cable fence. Jessie barked, walking over to the cow, crouching like an attacking coyote. She looked like a miniature cutting horse, maneuvering the cows around the pen. Then she ran full speed, barking with her strong, clear voice, causing the baby longhorn to dart across the arena toward the open gate. Jessie ran beside it the whole way, preventing it from changing course. The moment the calf ran through the gate, Jessie stopped, barked one last time, and then began walking back toward the house.

My jaw dropped.

"Did Jessie understand everything we were saying?" I asked in awe.

Mom laughed. "It sure looks like it!"

Jessie finally made it back to us, panting from the heat. Although she looked hot and exhausted, I couldn't help but see the proud and invigorated look in her eyes.

"Good girl, Jessie!" Mom cried, bending down and kissing her little red head. "You're better than any trained cow dog!"

Just as I opened my mouth to praise Jessie as well, someone shouted, "Hello!"

"Mom?" Mom asked, spinning around. Indeed, Mimi was walking into our yard, carrying bags of takeout. Grandpa followed behind her, fiddling with his baseball cap that read "West Point."

"Hello!" Mimi sang again.

"What in the world are you two doing here?" Mom asked, looking exhausted.

"Well, I thought I would bring some dinner and make sure you two aren't malnourished, living out here in the middle of nowhere," Mimi said, lifting up shopping bags filled with barbecue.

"I told her everything was fine," Grandpa said. "I told her that two strong women like you could survive out here on a ranch, let alone feed yourselves."

I checked my wristwatch. "Dinner, at three o'clock?"

"Well, I don't like to drive in the dark, so I came out here early so I could get home before the sun starts to set," Mimi explained as Mom and I approached.

"Sounds fine to me," I said as wafting scents of barbecue entered my nose. "Hi, Mimi. Hi, Grandpa." I gave them both hugs.

"Well, I don't think barbecue is exactly the most nourishing thing," Mom said.

"I know, Emily. I told Maurice that, but he insisted on bringing barbecue. I brought salads from Whole Foods as well."

I gave Grandpa a silent "Thank you," and he nodded.

"Let's not dillydally about. My makeup is going to melt off in this heat," Mimi sighed, leading the way to the house. "Snap to it, Maurice."

Once we were all inside, I helped myself to a barbecued hamburger, took a small amount of salad to pacify Mimi, and sat down at the table.

"Shall we say a blessing?" Mom asked as she looked at Grandpa to her left and then at Mimi and me to her right.

"Sure, you say it, Mom," I said, clasping Mimi's hand and reaching for Grandpa, who sat on the opposite end of the table. It was a mighty long reach, but I managed.

Mom blessed the food and crossed herself when she finished—she always crosses herself after prayers even though we aren't Catholic. After the blessing, I resumed my seat and scooted my chair into the table. "Nothing like a barbecued hamburger," I said before sinking my teeth into the warm bun.

"It's fully cooked, right?" Mimi asked as she held hers up to the light while looking at me from the corner of her eye.

"No, the restaurant gave her meat that was oozing blood. Yes, it's well done. They wouldn't dare give *you* anything that was even questionable," Grandpa said through a mouthful of barbecue beans.

"I wasn't asking you," Mimi chimed as she looked at Grandpa and then to me. I quickly inspected my hamburger patty.

"I do not find a trace of pinkness in my hamburger," I said, looking at Mimi. I resumed eating.

"You know the way I used to eat my steaks?" Grandpa asked as he chewed on a huge bite of baked potato.

"How?" Mom asked. We both had heard this story so many times.

"Cook it on one side for a minute and then the other for thirty seconds. It's perfect," he said, very proud of his style of cooking. "When I drove through Alaska in my RV, I used to get my steaks from Costco—the best steaks I've ever had."

"Costco stores are everywhere, Maurice. I don't think Alaskan Costco steaks are any better than Texas Costco steaks."

"They certainly are!"

"Besides, a steak is different than hamburger meat. Hamburgers have to be well done," Mimi said as she kept her eyes fixed upon a stubborn bean that was sliding around her plate. "E. coli," she added.

"I like my meat rare," Grandpa replied, obviously just being stubborn.

"Oh, guess what I heard on the news today," Mimi said suddenly, as if it were an urgent matter. She leaned forward to emphasize the importance of the matter.

"I give up. What is it?" I said sarcastically as I gave Grandpa a half smirk, half smile.

"A new study came out that said if you flush an airplane toilet while sitting, it will suction you to the seat and you won't be able to get back up. A lady was stuck on the toilet for a whole plane ride because she flushed the toilet while she was on it. Can you believe that? Wouldn't that be horrible?" Mimi said. By the look on her face, you would have thought California had fallen into the Pacific Ocean.

"Lorraine, I have been a pilot all my life and I have never heard of that happening," Grandpa sighed.

"Well, I trust the news."

"That would be horrible," Mom confessed as she ate a piece of lettuce. She was having a dry hamburger patty and a salad. I looked at my plate, which was overflowing with barbecue beans and a barbecued hamburger. *Just for today,* I thought as I dug my teeth into my disappearing burger.

"Also, get this—" Mimi started.

"This is Mount McKinley in Alaska. I took the picture when I was flying my propeller plane over it," Grandpa suddenly said, interrupting Mimi midbreath. We all turned our heads rapidly to face Grandpa, wondering whether he was hallucinating or had just plumb lost it. Neither of our assumptions was correct. He was holding up the new iPad we had purchased for him. A clear picture of Mount McKinley was on the screen.

"Wow, that's a great photo, Dad," Mom said as she nodded slowly.

"Maurice, I was talking," Mimi said, tilting her head sideways.

"You're so beautiful, Lorraine," Grandpa said. "No wonder I can't ever eat at the table."

Mimi smirked. "What do you want now, Maurice?"

"See that picture over there on your piano?" Grandpa asked, pointing to the picture of Mimi and Grandpa on their wedding night, where they looked so happy together. "It's been downhill ever since." He winked at me.

"Dad, you just ruined your compliment with that statement. Stop when you're ahead," Mom said, rolling her eyes and smiling at Grandpa. He chuckled and lowered his iPad, unfazed, and began to look at his screen again, tapping it once in a while.

"Anyway, as I was *about* to say, I am selling a house to this cute young girl, but she has *five* dogs . . ."

"Wow, she sounds like us," I said. I looked over at Chubbs, who was silently climbing down from the couch with her dog bowl in her mouth. She made her way over to the table, dropping the dog bowl with a loud clang at Mimi's feet, causing her to yelp.

"Dog, shoo, shoo, I'm allergic to you. Shoo, shoo!" Mimi said, waving her arm.

"Oh, Mom, she just wants a pat," Mom said. Mimi grudgingly reached down and tapped her on the head with two fingers, then shooed her once more. Chubbs gave up and walked away.

"You know I'm allergic to those dogs," Mimi said, straightening the napkin in her lap. "I can't help it! I love them, but they just make me sneeze."

"I think they are allergic to you," Grandpa whispered. He cupped his hands over his mouth and faced me, silently mouthing, "She's not allergic." Thankfully, Mimi didn't catch it and continued on with her story.

"Most neighborhoods do not allow more than three dogs." Mimi said. "I had to look here, there, and yonder for a nice neighborhood that would allow her to bring all of her dogs." She took a deep breath and released it heavily.

"Poor Mommy, such a good Realtor," Mom said as she patted Mimi on the back, talking like she was addressing a little child.

"Oh," Mimi sighed again. "But nothing is as bad as what your brother is going through," she began, her mood totally changing as she sat up straight once more.

"Here is a moose in downtown Anchorage," Grandpa piped up again as he held up his iPad. "It was in the middle of Main Street." Grandpa has always loved everything Alaska. He has said that Alaska is the only place he would ever live—other than Texas, of course.

I laughed at the sound of pride in Grandpa's voice as he showed off his pictures.

"Maurice, I am trying to tell a story, dear," Mimi said.

"Oh, sorry, I thought you were finished," Grandpa said as he lowered his iPad and resumed surfing through his photo gallery.

"Anyway . . . Where was I?"

"This is Portage Glacier," Grandpa said.

"That's a great picture, Grandpa. Where did you take it from?"

"My RV, I think. Or I might have been jogging on one of the many trails."

"Hello, I'm still talking!"

"Your story is sure taking a long time." Grandpa scowled.

"I'm almost finished. Okay, so your brother was showing a house last month—"

Grandpa blew his nose loudly into his napkin.

"Maurice! How many times have I told you it is improper to blow your nose at the table!" Mimi interrupted herself this time.

Grandpa looked at Mimi like he was a teasing two-year-old and blew his nose a second time. Mimi glanced down at her plate, pressing her mouth together. She forked some potato salad and shoved it into her mouth. Her irritation showed most in her chewing. I turned my head and gave Grandpa a wide-eyed glance. *Oops,* I thought.

"You need to learn to say 'Yes, dear,' Dad. It would get you a lot farther in life," Mom said.

"What happened to Uncle Tom?" I asked quietly.

"Oh, never mind. Grandpa obviously doesn't want to hear the story."

"You already told me about it!" Grandpa exclaimed.

"I want to know what happened," I said.

"Well, this one house Tom was showing was filled with monkeys! The people had *pet monkeys*! One of the monkeys walked up to him and climbed all the way up to his arm, then started to swing on it! Can you imagine? It must have been horrifying! Tom said the place smelled like a sewer too. I can only imagine the trouble it is going to be to fix that place up," Mimi said as she finished her story.

"I bet you anything those people are experimenting on their pets," Mom said.

"What are we supposed to do? Call the police or something? I really can't believe those people have not been caught already," Mimi exclaimed.

"Well, that is quite a story, Mimi," I said as I shuddered at the thought of a monkey-infested house.

"How is work, Dad?" Mom asked Grandpa. "Now it is his turn to talk," she added, looking at Mimi.

"Oh, it's okay. I'm working in the flight simulator all next week, every day starting at five a.m. I have this one student I have to send back to training. I'm getting a lot of heat for it, but he crashed three times! That is just unforgivable," Grandpa said.

"Do you think your potato is salted enough?" I heard Mimi whisper in my ear.

"Yes, it's fine," I whispered back.

"Shh! Grandpa is talking now," Mom said.

"I was just asking Jules if she needed more salt. I think my potato tastes very bland. I'm going to get some salt," Mimi said as she rose from the table. I shrugged to Mom, who was looking at me.

"Oh! There is a West Point football game at the Southern Methodist University stadium in November. I already bought tickets," Grandpa said.

"Oh, yay! We'll be there," I said. Grandpa was never very active in any West Point activities. The only reunion he'd attended was his fiftieth—and Mom had made us all go.

"When in November?" Mom asked.

"I don't know. I don't have the tickets in front of me. Sometime in early November, I think," Grandpa said as he continued munching on potato salad.

"You know," Mimi began, "November is the beginning of winter. It will be very cold. It might be sleeting!" she finished in a very matter-of-fact tone.

"Mom!" Mom shouted. "Let's do a little experiment. Let's see if you two can say one nice thing about each other. Dad, you go first."

"Why do I have to go first?" Grandpa whined. Mom gave him the look. He was deep in thought for a second, and it turned into a long, silent pause. I suddenly got nervous that our lunch was going to fall apart if Grandpa said something naughty. "Lorraine will always be there for you if you are sick and in the hospital, and she will take care of you."

"There, a nice thing to say! Wasn't that nice, Mom?" Mom asked. Mimi let out an "Mm-hm" and looked at her plate. "Now it's your turn to say something nice about Dad."

Mimi became very interested in the last remaining bean on her plate and studied it thoroughly. There was another long pause, longer than the first.

"He is a good pilot," Mimi said quickly.

"That's it?" Mom asked.

"That was a very nice compliment!" Mimi said defensively.

Mom rolled her eyes and looked at me.

"Who wants some ice cream?" Mimi asked as she pushed back her chair to stand up.

Grandpa shot up his hand. "Me!"

"You haven't finished your dilled green beans yet, Maurice. You can't have ice cream," Mimi said. "Jules, would you like some?"

"I'm stuffed!" I said. "Well, maybe I'll have a little bit," I added sluggishly.

"Jules hasn't finished all her green beans yet!" Grandpa shouted. "I finished my entire hamburger."

"This was actually my second helping," I whispered to myself.

"Mom, he can have some ice cream," Mom said to Mimi, who was now hovering over my plate and was about to pick it up.

"He has not been eating well for the past few days. All he has had to eat is potato chips and crackers and ice cream. I tried to give him pasta and meat loaf, but he never touched either," Mimi said defensively.

"That's not true! I ate at Whataburger for lunch yesterday," Grandpa put in.

"And what did you have there?"

"A milk shake," Grandpa said slyly.

"Exactly my—"

"He can have some ice cream! Come on, Mom. Really?" Mom said.

"Fine. I give up trying to make him good meals," Mimi said.

"They aren't any good anyway," Grandpa muttered as he resumed surfing through pictures.

"O-o-okay. Let's help Mimi with the dishes," Mom said as she stood up. I noticed her body conveniently blocked Grandpa from Mimi's ferocious stare.

"You know, you never cease to amaze me, Emily," Grandpa said as he picked up the book Mom wrote, which had been laying on the table beside him.

"Well, thank you, Dad. That means a lot to me," Mom said as she folded her napkin onto her plate and stacked her silverware on top. She smiled, genuinely touched, kissing Grandpa on the forehead.

"Just like your mother, she works so hard—such a great work ethic—and she is so beautiful for seventy-two," Grandpa said, looking at Mom. Mom quickly whirled her head to Mimi.

"Wow!" Mom said, aghast. "It is not every day you hear a comment like that coming from Dad. We should have gotten that on tape."

I laughed at Mimi's face as she widened her eyes. "Well, thank you, Maurice," Mimi said as she dropped the dishes into the sink with a clang. "What do you want in return now?" She smirked at me. I stood, picked up my plate, and, walking over to Mimi, whispered, "A simple thank you is sufficient."

"I just want to be able to sit in bed and listen to the television with my headphones," Grandpa said as he placed his napkin on his plate.

"You don't let him do that, Mom?" Mom asked, her jaw dropping.

"She won't let me watch television with my head-phones, yet she always falls to sleep with the TV *blaring* and all the lights on."

"Now, now," Mimi started. "When you come to bed at two in the morning and decide to watch television, it wakes me up and then I can't go back to sleep for *hours*. Also, I've read that the television actually keeps you up at night and disrupts your sleep patterns." Mimi began putting the dishes in the dishwasher. "Oh my!" she suddenly exclaimed. "The sun is already setting! I won't make it home before it gets dark now. Maurice, hop to it, we have to run."

"Can I stay here?" Grandpa asked, looking up at me with puppy eyes from his chair. I smiled and gave him a hug.

"I don't think that would go over very well with Mimi," I whispered.

"You're right. She needs me . . . but she'd never admit it."

"Maurice," Mimi said, "you're going to lose your ride if you don't snap to it."

"Well, thanks for bringing dinner, Mom," Mom said, walking over to Mimi and giving her a hug.

"Hey, the barbecue was my idea!" Grandpa exclaimed.

"Thank you too, Dad." Mom smiled, hugging Grandpa.

Soon they were out the door, Mimi's little white Mercedes zooming down the gravel road, gone as quickly as they had arrived.

"Well, that was fun," I laughed. Mom rolled her eyes.

"Let's go feed the horses," Mom said as the setting sun filled the house with a warm glow.

It always amazed me how quickly the sun set. One moment it would be brushing the tops of the trees and the next it was completely gone, twilight covering the land. By the time we reached the barn, everything was foggy in the light of dusk. All the horses whinnied at the top of their lungs, anxious for dinner. I ran over to Rocky's stall, swinging open the door to give him a huge embrace. "How are you doing, Rocky boy?" His ears perked to attention as he playfully bit my shirtsleeve, pulling on it. I flinched, thankful he hadn't decided to take my skin along with the fabric. I could never imagine Rocky biting me, though; he was too sweet. I knew all he wanted was a treat.

"I don't have anything. Sorry, buddy. You have already had six carrots today! Now please let go of my shirt . . . Right now would be preferable," I said as I tapped his nose gently. He jerked his head back and dropped my shirt. "Thank you," I said, stroking his long, black neck before I walked away.

"*Jules!*" Mom yelled in a panicked voice.

That's not good. Mom's tone said everything with only that single word: someone was hurt. I tried to follow Mom's voice and dashed into Maggie's stall, my feet sliding from under me on the fresh shavings. When I got there, I didn't see a single soul. I regained my balance and ran out to her pasture. Then I stopped.

Mom was standing in the middle of the pasture, looking not at me but at Maggie, who stood in the line of trees inside the pasture. I could tell something was very wrong by the way she stood, standing strangely erect but motionless. My heart skipped a beat. I ran full speed, halting next to Mom. She stared at me and then took off toward Maggie, dropping to her knees next to the horse's legs.

Maggie radiated an aura of distress. She was rocked back, like a slightly tilting marble statue, so all of her weight was on her back two legs, in a noticeable attempt to alleviate pain originating in the front of her body. Mom pressed her hands firmly onto Maggie's front hooves; I knew from Mom's lessons on horse care that she was trying to find if her hooves were radiating heat. If they were, then that meant founder, which happened when the horse's hoof bone rotated downward. The amount of rotation depended on the severity of the founder. I could tell by the way Mom quickly let go of Maggie's hoof that a great amount of heat was coming from it.

Mom whispered words under her breath about a farrier, apparently talking to the patch of grass beside her. I stood nervously, looking at Mom, whose face was becoming more and more concerned.

"Call the vet," Mom said. I tried to keep a clear mind as I watched Maggie keep her neck tightly erect, causing the powerful muscles to show through the delicate skin of her coat. The slow, powerful grinding of her teeth indicated the pain she was experiencing. Then Maggie bent her head down and nuzzled Mom's chest, sending Mom off balance a little. "Tell the vet it looks like severe founder and that her front left hoof is hot and inflamed. Jules, she is in a lot of pain. Tell them to come quickly." Mom looked up at me with a look of worry that overrode the current of panic surging through her eyes.

I bit my lip, turned, and ran full speed, using all of the strength left in me to sprint through the weedy uphill trek to the barn. Clamoring into the barn, my snake boots clattered against the floor with resounding force. R2 whinnied upon my entrance. She seemed to sense that I was feeling panicked and distressed.

"It's okay, R2," I said as I ran by. I snatched Mom's phone off the dusty, rusty, ancient barn stereo. A film of sticky dust had already accumulated on the phone, particles lodged in the crevices of the speaker. I rubbed furiously on the screen to peel off the dust and succeeded in removing a small circle's worth, just enough to see the keypad.

Our whole ranch was a notorious dead spot for cell service, especially in the barn. I saw the detested words pop up on the screen in front of me: *No Service*. I ran to the top of the hill outside the barn, where the phone received one bar of service if you stood on the right amount of toes and held your breath for the right amount of time. I swirled the phone around in the air impatiently. No service bars appeared, no small ray of service floated past my phone in the still air. Everything around me darkened as night set in. I could just barely make out the outline of the barn, the tree line, and Mom's faint figure bent beside Maggie.

The palms of my hands were sweating, and my toe tapped on a gravel rock impatiently. My brain also seemed to be out of service, refusing to remind me of how to simply dial a number on the keypad. I stared blankly at the screen for a solid minute. Finally, a small bar of service popped up, and with it a wisp of consciousness arrived and reminded me the vet was in the speed dial list.

"Please answer, please answer," I whispered under my breath, tapping my toe. I looked over at Mom, who was still bent over Maggie's suffering figure. The phone seemed to ring at an artificially sluggish pace, the dial tone sounding like a long, vibrating belch in my ear. I heard a small click on the line, and I moved the phone away from my ear and peered at the dark screen. I saw that it read someone had answered.

"Hello?" I asked, my voice sounding stressed and uneasy.

"Large Animal Clinic in Creek View, this is Missy," the slightly annoyed, drawling country voice answered in a nonchalant tone.

"Um, hi," I sputtered. I wanted to at least squeak a sound so she wouldn't hang up the phone. I forced myself to go on in a calmer tone of voice. "We have an apparent case of severe founder out here on our ranch. Our palomino is rocked back, pushing her weight onto her hindquarters, shifting it. She is in a lot of pain. We need a vet to come out right away," I said. "I mean, very quickly."

"Yes, well, the doctor on call is in surgery right now. He won't be out for four hours," Missy stated, showing no feeling, hanging on to the note at the end of the last word as if she were about to add something else to her nonexpressive sentence.

"But?" I asked.

"Oh, there isn't a 'but.'" I heard a heavy exhale on the other side of the line.

"That won't work. Her feet are hot, she is grinding her teeth because of the amount of pain . . . Which vet can be here the soonest?" I gave her our address.

"Please hold," Missy said. I gasped as I heard a click in the receiver and realized that I was possibly on hold for an endless amount of time.

I was in true torture. I could not pace, because then I would lose service. I could not doodle on anything since I was standing in the middle of the road. I could only stare at Maggie and Mom, stare at the specks of living beings in the distance. I bit my lip as time ticked by, with no sound on the other end of the line. I was just about to check and see if I had lost connection when I heard Missy take my phone off hold.

"Dr. Shilo can probably be out at your place the soonest. I will have him call you, maybe . . . well . . . I think he can be there in twenty minutes. He was dropping off some medication to a ranch that is not far from y'all." I heard Missy typing something into what I guessed was an electronic device in the vet clinic.

"Perfect. Thank you so much," I said, running through the mental checklist of what Mom had ordered me to say to the clinic. It seemed I had forgotten something, but I couldn't quite remember what it was . . . "Oh! Missy," I cried as the last item on my checklist thrust through the hallways of my mind. "Please tell Dr. Shilo that our gate code is 1122 and to close it behind him. It does not close automatically and we have cows loose."

"Okay. Thank you."

I firmly pressed down on the flaming red End button on the screen and then locked the phone, sliding it into the back pocket of my jeans. Glancing over to Maggie's pasture, I bit the side of my lip and clenched my hands. Through the darkness I could barely see Mom walking toward Maggie with a halter. I said a quick prayer, looking into the sky. I cried out to a presence that I felt standing right beside me, trying to comfort me—an invisible spirit—asking it to take away Maggie's pain.

I saw Mom begin to lead Maggie into the barn. I breathed in deeply and then shot off down the hill through the darkness and into the barn again.

"Does she have any history with founder?" Dr. Shilo asked as he listened to Maggie's heartbeat. He stood somewhat hunched, holding a stethoscope to Maggie's slightly heaving chest, his red hair rubbing up against Maggie's coat. Maggie convulsed her skin to shake off a fly, or what she thought was a fly but was actually Dr. Shilo's hand.

The fluorescent lights buzzed incessantly above us, interrupted only by the clink of beetles as they slammed into the lightbulbs. I flicked a beetle off my shirt, trying to very quickly overcome my irrational phobia of June bugs.

"Yes, she often goes lame when she is shod," Mom said as she nervously stroked Maggie's flank. Suddenly Mom's entire face changed. "Oh no. The farrier was just out here a few days ago. He has always known how delicate Maggie's hooves are, but this last time he cut her back so far. I told him not to, but he did it anyway. Oh no. That farrier did this . . ."

"Her lungs and heart sound fine," Dr. Shilo said, ignoring Mom's spiel on the farrier. "Let's look at her hooves here." He squeezed Maggie from the shoulder down, as if looking for something in the deep crevices of Maggie's muscular legs.

He picked up her front left hoof by pressing on the joint above the heel of her hoof, then pressed a big, pliers-like contraption onto Maggie's sole. To my relief, she didn't appear to be extremely bothered by the pressure; she only wanted to put her foot back on the ground.

"She isn't that tender, which makes me wonder if this is just a severe stone bruise," Dr. Shilo said.

"I don't think a stone bruise would cause her this much pain," Mom said.

"If it was a founder, her sole would be much tenderer than it is right now."

A long silence ensued.

"What do we do to treat a stone bruise?" Mom asked, shooting me a look that told me she was not convinced of the vet's diagnosis.

"You will just soak her foot for ten minutes a day with Epsom salts," he said as he placed his hoof testers in his messy vet bag. It overflowed with bottles labeled with smeared Sharpie, long, grimy tubes that coiled like snakes, and empty shot syringes.

"You're not going to like that, now, are you, Maggie?" I whispered into her ear. Standing right by her face, I saw the look of concern in her intelligent eyes. She nudged me in the side with her nose, sending me falling back slightly. "Yeah. It's not that bad. We are going to make you feel better," I said as I stroked her face. I swirled my finger around the tiny silver spot at the very tip of her nose.

Mom continued to ask Dr. Shilo questions, but my ears drowned out their competing voices from my mind, blocking everything but my ability to see Maggie. I just concentrated on the beautiful creature before me. Maggie appeared to be trying to tell me something, though I couldn't decipher what it was. She looked straight at me, as if looking into my soul, twitching her ear back and then forward again in some kind of code. She was concerned, and wasn't feeling better. I tried to decipher the whole message of Maggie's pain by the one look that flashed through her eyes.

"Did you hear that, Jules?" Mom asked. "You're going to have to help me remember this."

"No, I'm sorry. Could you say that again?" I said while shaking my head, trying to snap into focus and look at Dr. Shilo.

"Get a bucket of mildly hot water, put about two hand-fuls of Epsom salts in it, and soak her hoof. I would give her two grams of Bute paste tonight, just to make her feel better and make you feel like you are doing something for her pain. I'll go get you a bag of salts from my car," hhe said, looking at me with his cold brown eyes. I didn't like the tone of his voice. For some reason, he didn't believe that Maggie was actually sick, instead acting like we were disrupting his evening. He picked up his bag and threw it over his shoulder. Mom and I looked at each other once he had left the barn.

"What is a stone bruise?" I asked Mom.

"What she doesn't have. I really think she is found-ering, and it's all because of that farrier," Mom replied, shaking her head.

"It's okay, Maggie. Tell us what's wrong," Mom said. Maggie stomped her left foot, the metal shoe striking the floor and leaving a mark. She could clearly understand us, but we wanted to understand her.

Dr. Shilo reentered the barn with a blue bag reading "Epsom Salts" in bold black letters. I saw the greasy-looking white rocks through the transparent top of the bag. I wondered how in the world this could be anything but a remedy for sore muscles.

"So should we start it tonight or in the morning?" I asked, just to clarify.

"In the morning is fine, but the Bute tonight," he said. "Go ahead and give me a shout if she gets worse or doesn't get any better by the day after tomorrow."

"Thank you, Dr. Shilo," Mom said as she slowly untied Maggie's lead rope. She curled the rope up in her hands, carefully turning Maggie around to walk her into her stall. Her limp was obvious and her head thrust downward on every second step she took, every step that applied pressure to the left hoof. A look of sadness and pain creased Mom's forehead as she watched her beloved Maggie.

I went to get the Bute paste from the cabinet in the feed room, then handed it to Mom and watched as she applied it tenderly to Maggie's hoof. Mom sniffed as she wiped a teardrop with the back of her plaid shirt.

"She'll be okay, Mom. She'll be okay," I said, taking her hand once she exited Maggie's stall.

"I just feel like we have to do something else!" Mom cried as she looked over at Maggie, who now stood looking out her stall window at the appearing stars. *Maggie loves looking through her window at her stars.* Standing in her twelve-by-twenty-four-foot stall, she looked like a queen looking out from her castle tower.

"Mom, you know you have done all you can for tonight."

A meow coming from the end of the barn scared me half to death. I momentarily panicked, thinking Sparkle had escaped the house. I looked at the end of the barn and saw a gray-and-black cat sitting at the back entrance of the barn. On closer inspection, I saw it had a white triangle on its chest in the shape of a bandana. *Definitely not Sparkle.*

"Hey, Mom," I said. "There's a cat in the barn."

"What now? I'm not keeping another pet," Mom said, looking away from Maggie.

"Well, look at it. It's hungry. Don't we have some extra cat food down here we could give it?" I asked.

"I guess we could feed it just for tonight," Mom sighed. I rummaged through the feed room and finally found a can of old cat food. I clicked open the can.

After much coaxing on my end, the cat followed me through the darkness to the little pasture beside the barn where we kept our wheelbarrows. I placed the cat food can right under a wheelbarrow and crouched down to watch the feral cat devour its food.

"What should we name it?" I asked.

"We aren't keeping it."

"It will keep coming around now that we gave it food."

Mom sighed. "It has a cute little bandana marking on it, so how about we call it Bandana?" Mom asked.

"I like it. What do you think, Bandana?" I asked the cat, who was too busy devouring the food to answer. "Is it a boy or girl?"

"Can't tell," Mom answered. "It's too dark."

I always loved watching cats eat. When I listened closely, they made a little quiet sound from deep in their throats that sounded like they were saying, *"Yum, yum."* Well, at least my cats did. Bandana was thoroughly enjoying his meal when all of a sudden he looked up, froze like he saw something really cool, then looked back down and continued eating. I thought I had seen something too; it looked almost like a butterfly. *But butterflies don't usually come out at night.* I shrugged. *Mysterious ranch.*

"Help me!" I suddenly heard Mom scream.

"What in the world?" I cried, spinning to face Mom. She didn't have to answer—it was obvious she was being attacked by a bat. The creature was flying right toward her face like her nose was its landing strip. And it was *huge.*

"Ah!" Mom yelped as she ran in circles, flailing her arms around. She started spinning her arms around her face so fast she knocked her glasses off her nose. I watched them spiral through the air in slow motion, the moonlight glinting off the lenses, before they landed straight in a pile of knee-high weeds. The bat still followed her.

"I can't *see!*" Mom yelled as she blindly grabbed hold of my hand and whisked me away, dragging me into the barn while waving one arm in front of her.

"What was that, what was that, what *was that*?" Mom exclaimed, collapsing into the rocking chair. She is pretty much blind as a bat—yes, a bat—when she doesn't have her glasses on, so she squinted at me as she talked, waving her arms in front of her to try to figure out where I was.

"Well, it was a bat. I thought it was a butterfly when I first saw it . . ."

"A bat? It was a *bat*? You saw it and didn't say anything?" Mom asked, panicked.

"Well, it all happened so fast that when I turned to tell you that I saw something, it was already in your face."

"A *bat*! Oh my gosh, oh my gosh," Mom said. "Did it bite me? It could have rabies! Oh my gosh! Do you see a bite mark? Did it really touch me or was it just hovering in front of me? Are you sure there are no bite marks?" Mom said, pulling back her hair to expose her hairline and bending down for me to examine for a bite mark.

"Mom, you would know if a bat bit you," I said, examining her forehead.

"Just, do you see anything?" Mom said nervously. She coughed twice.

"I'm looking, I'm looking," I said as I thoroughly inspected her face. "Nope, nothing."

"Okay, okay," Mom said as she leaned forward in the rocking chair. She felt her pulse on the side of her neck. "My heart's racing. I think I'm in a-fib."

"You're just frightened. It's all okay. You weren't bitten by a bat."

"Are you sure?" she added, about to pull back her hair again.

"I'm positive. Plus, you would have felt it. Can we go to the house now before we have any more close encounters of the second kind?"

"Yeah. Let's go," Mom said as she stood up a little wobbly.

"Wait!" I said. Mom jumped. "Don't you need your glasses?"

"Don't I have another pair in the house?" Mom said desperately, obviously not wanting to go back over to the scene of the horror. She looked very tired.

"I don't think so," I said. "Come on, let's at least go look. I think I know where they are."

Mom and I cautiously walked back to the side of the barn, looking for any signs of movement. The moon was now behind a cloud, so we really couldn't see a thing. It appeared Bandana had finished dinner and was now gone.

"I found them," I finally whispered, seeing the glint of the metal through the weeds. I handed them to Mom and she put them on her nose. They were a little crooked.

"I think we need to get them fixed." I laughed, trying to adjust the glasses on her nose.

"No, right now I am going to bed."

"And my first day of school is tomorrow," I reminded Mom. I thought she might faint on me. I was suddenly very worried.

"I almost forgot. Hurry up, come on! We have to get you in bed. You have to wash your hair and get all this sweat off you. And we have to get all of your uniforms ready. I have to make sure you have all the books you need packed up in your book bag. What am I going to fix for breakfast?" I was immediately sorry I had mentioned anything.

"We have to figure out exactly how long it takes to get to school, what time we have to leave . . ."

SIX

The GPS says we should be there by now," Mom said.
If that's the case, I'm going to school in a field of sunflowers.
Acres of sunflowers—and nothing but sunflowers—
extended out on either side of the isolated two-lane road
as far as the eye could see.

"Your destination is ahead on the right," the GPS
chimed. There was nothing on the right.

"Just keep driving a bit," I suggested. "Sometimes the
GPS is a few miles off."

Mom continued driving, peering out the windshield,
hoping to see a school building magically appear in the field.
To make matters worse, we drove due east, which meant the
sun blared straight into the car, nearly blinding me every
time I tried to watch the road. After a few miles, we arrived
at a four-way stop. A single flashing light hung in the center,
precariously supported by very old, tattered wiring.

No one else was on the road. Mom and I sat at the
four-way stop for a moment, trying to collect our thoughts
and figure out where we were. A rusty windmill creaked
in the wind to our right. *Does my school even exist?* I began
to fear that the pictures I had seen on the Web were taken
in some bygone era and now all that remained were . . .
sunflowers.

Then, suddenly, as if a magic clock struck twelve,
civilization appeared, or at least some form of it: three

mammoth pickup trucks barreled toward the intersection from our left. The first truck in line nearly scraped the bottom of the rickety flashing light as it roared in front of us across the intersection. A two-foot gap spanned between the top of the tires and the bottom of the truck bed. As it passed in front of us, I couldn't even see the windows on the doors. I felt like an ant next to a Tyrannosaurus rex.

The next two trucks were more reasonably sized, but one had longhorn horns attached to the grill. The other was completely covered in mud, making me wonder if the driver had driven through a lake to get here.

"Should we follow them?" I asked feebly, as the last of the three trucks disappeared behind the sunflowers on the right. Mom nodded silently.

Turning the car to the right, Mom followed the three pickups along an unnecessarily windy road. Deciding to check the rearview mirror, I found that at least a dozen cars were now on the road behind us—all of them were pickups. I felt increasingly out of place in our midsized SUV.

Still, nothing appeared on the landscape except for sunflowers. Then, suddenly, the sunflower fields changed to evenly mowed grass, and a huge football stadium towered into the sky. I couldn't help but feel I had just entered into a scene from *Field of Dreams*.

The stadium was bigger than my entire school complex in New York City. The bleachers easily surpassed three stories in height, and the field extended back into the property past my range of vision. *They never offered football in New York City. Maybe it's a Texas thing.*

"I think we found it," Mom said. The stadium morphed into a single-story school building complex that sprawled out over a five-acre lot. Four different buildings were linked together by covered walkways. The buildings edged a long, circular gravel drive encasing three flagpoles: a Texas flag, an American flag, and a large blue-and-white flag reading "Creek View Christian Academy." We pulled into the carpool line, which snaked around the circle drive, quickly growing longer and longer as more pickup trucks pulled in behind us. A white Cadillac pickup truck pushed its way into the carpool line in front of us. Glistening in the sun, the truck's pearly white body was spotless; it looked brand-new except for a gun rack that hung above the truck bed. Two dogs ran around in the truck bed, peering out over the sides and yapping at all the commotion. They looked like pit bulls.

As we inched closer and closer to the main building, my phone vibrated in my lap.

"Mimi's calling," I said to Mom.

"Go ahead and answer. She probably wants to wish you a good first day of school."

I pressed the green Talk button on my phone. "Hello?"

"Oh hi!" Mimi yelled—she was obviously in her car and had me on speaker. She never could figure out that the microphone was located right above the driver seat and that yelling was unnecessary. "Are you almost to school?"

"Actually, we just arrived. We are in the carpool line now."

"Good! Well, I won't keep you long," Mimi began, still screaming, "but I just wanted to wish you the best of luck on your first day at a new school!"

"Thank you, Mimi."

"Oh! Guess what!"

"What?"

"I was just listening to NPR on my radio and I heard that they recently discovered a translucent spider that hides under the rim of toilet seats. They've found them in public restrooms, and since you're going to that school in the middle of God knows where, I suggest that you check the toilet thoroughly before using the restroom. They are extremely poisonous and several people have been taken to the hospital because of the bites and died—"

"All right, Lorraine, that's enough. Stop bombarding her with that nonsense." Grandpa's voice suddenly boomed through the telephone. He was apparently driving around with Mimi. "Jules, honey, don't worry about spiders. Just have a nice first day of school. I know you will love it."

My mind filled with images of translucent spiders, massive pickup trucks, and endless fields of sunflowers.

"Is everything okay?" Mom asked, looking at my stunned face. I nodded.

"Okay, thanks, Mimi and Grandpa," I said. "I think I'm next in the carpool line."

"Well, have a great day! Call us on your way home!" Mimi chimed.

"Love you, sweetheart," Grandpa said.

"Bye-bye now," Mimi said.

"You're going to love your new school," Grandpa added. "Check out the football team!" Grandpa had been a high school football star and had played for West Point.

"Maybe you can even be a cheerleader!" Mimi called. After all, she had been a high school beauty queen.

They were obviously each trying to have the last word.

"Love you both. Talk to you soon." I lowered the phone and ended the call. Before I could ask Mom if she had heard of the translucent spider that hid underneath toilet seats, we approached the main building.

"All right, we are almost to drop-off," Mom said, smiling with excitement. "You have your book bag?"

My nondescript, gray rolling backpack was at my feet, next to my empty snake boots. Mom had insisted on ordering a rolling backpack for me—in order to "save my back"—and further insisted on ordering the free name engraving that came with the backpack. Unfortunately, there was no mistaking that the behemoth belonged to Jules O'Connor.

"You have your phone and your lunch box?"

I nodded. I zipped my phone into the front pocket of my backpack and retrieved my black lunch box from the seat behind me. It was already dripping with melting ice. Before I could say anything, however, the Cadillac in front of us threw on the brakes—we had arrived. Kids swarmed around the sidewalks.

"Do you want me to walk you to the door?" Mom asked, eager to help.

"I'm a big girl now, Mom," I said, smirking. I opened the door and hopped out, lugging my rolling backpack behind me, swinging the lunch box over my shoulder. The air smelled like diesel fuel and freshly cut grass.

In front of me, a tall, strapping man walked around his car and opened the passenger door of the pearly white Cadillac truck we had been following. He wore starched jeans, an ironed white button-down shirt, a gold belt buckle the size of my hand, and a cowboy hat. Looking over at me, he flashed a grin that reminded me of the picture of George Strait I had seen on Mom's album covers at the ranch.

"Thank you, Daddy." A high-pitched, southern belle voice emanated from the passenger seat of the truck. A tall, slender girl glided out of the car, shaking long blonde curls that softly cascaded down her back. A large, hot-pink headband held the hair away from her face, revealing her perfect profile. I suddenly felt self-conscious about my frizzy ponytail I had brushed into place while in the car.

"You're welcome, Minnie. Anything for my princess," the man cooed, kissing the girl on the top of the head. "Have a great first day at your new school." The man waved at me as he walked back to his car, tipping his cowboy hat. I still stood in the same spot on the sidewalk next to Mom's car.

As Minnie turned to wave to her father, she made eye contact with me. Upon seeing my stupefied stare, she looked at me with the same expression a person would give a homeless dog. She used her long fingernails, which matched the color of her headband, to brush back a golden lock of hair. It was safe to say Minnie was my polar opposite. Her face was covered in the perfect blend of makeup: blue eyeliner accentuated her light blue eyes, rosy blush highlighted her strong cheekbones, mascara lengthened her already voluminous eyelashes, and her lips were tinted just the slightest shade of red. I, on the other hand, wore no makeup—just as I had pretty much every day in New York City.

Minnie's uniform also greatly surpassed mine, which further dumbfounded me since I thought all uniforms were the same. Her uniform skirt was secured tightly around her small waist and flared out perfectly—unlike mine, which fell with absolutely no shape whatsoever over my nondescript waist and hips. She wore ankle socks that peeked out above shoes that accentuated her tan legs and petite feet. Looking down at my feet, I found hefty tennis shoes that were at least a size too large. My white ribbed kneesocks nearly touched the hem of my skirt, which was an inch longer than the required length—unlike Minnie's, which I could tell was at least two inches too short for the uniform code.

"Do you need help finding something?" a voice asked from behind me. I turned to find a woman who looked like she had walked off the set of the television show *Friday Night Lights*: she wore a light blue, full-skirted sundress and cowboy boots, her hair coiffed to perfection around her made-up face.

I blinked several times before realizing she had asked a question. "No, no . . . I mean, yes . . . You see, I'm new to the school, and . . ."

"Oh, honey bunches, you just follow me. My name is Lynette. My son is in the sixth grade, but he is already inside, playin' around with his friends." She laughed and clapped me on the shoulder, dragging me along with her. The wheels of my rolling backpack thumped loudly as they hit each groove in the cement sidewalk.

As we grew closer to the door, more mothers appeared around me as they walked their children into school, looking just like Lynette. *Maybe Mom should have walked me to the door.* Most children, however, walked in with their fathers, many of whom wore business suits, large belt buckles that reflected the morning sun, and cowboy boots.

Where am I?

Somehow I lost Lynette and ended up standing right beside Minnie. She smelled like roses and gardenias. Sniffing my shirt, I could only smell a lingering scent of dog and horse hair mixed with hay.

"Hello there, girls!" A loud voice resonated from my right. I turned and found a woman wearing a name tag that read "Mrs. Jackson, Middle School Principal." A denim dress hugged her slightly curvy figure and was accentuated by a large turquoise-and-leather belt that matched her turquoise boots. Her long, bleached-blonde hair was teased to such an extent that it stood three inches off the top of her head before falling to her shoulders like Dolly Parton's—even Mimi would have been proud. "What are y'all's names?"

I was quite unsure to whom she was referring.

"My name is Minnie Cooper," Minnie said in her beautiful Texas accent.

"I'm Jules O'Connor," I stammered.

"Oh! You two must be the two new students we have in the sixth grade!" She took Minnie and me by the shoulders and pulled us out of the flow of people.

"Now, I know how hard it is to be the new students," Mrs. Jackson said, accentuating the word *know*. Her dangling turquoise earrings bobbed back and forth as she nodded her head. "But rest assured, I am here for you both. If ever, ever you need anything, know that my door is open for you." I stole a glance at Minnie to see if she was as confused as I was. She was not. Instead, Minnie nodded her head back and forth gratefully, batting her long eyelashes.

"You know what, girls," Mrs. Jackson said, her eyes opening wide as she pressed her hand against her chest as if having a religious revelation. "I'm feeling called to pray over you. Dear Lord . . ." I quickly closed my eyes as Mrs. Jackson placed her hand on my head. "Protect these two girls today as they start their wonderful journey here at Creek View Christian Academy. Help them to make great new friends . . ." In all her fervor, Mrs. Jackson pressed harder and harder on my head. "And guide them through their studies and train them to be your disciples in this wild world. Amen!"

"Thank you so much, Mrs. Jackson. I feel so much better already knowing I'm with people who love the Lord as much as I do," Minnie cried.

Mrs. Jackson smiled and then looked at me expectantly.

"Oh yes, um, thank you so much. I can't wait," I said, trying to find the right words.

"Now, you two, go find your homeroom! Take the first hallway on your right, and it is the second room after you pass the library," Mrs. Jackson concluded, pushing us back into the flow of people who still marched through the doorway.

Well, she's no Mrs. Omega.

Much to my relief, Minnie walked ahead of me, leaving me behind to maneuver my rolling backpack around the feet of parents who stood chatting in the hallways. Finally, I reached the room. The class was evenly split between boys and girls, a shock in and of itself coming from an all-girls school. As I made my way through the desks, I saw a thirtysomething woman standing at the front of the room talking to a handful of students.

Someone tapped my shoulder. Spinning around, I found a girl with silky, shoulder-length brown hair smiling at me with an outstretched hand. She also wore a hint of makeup and a stylish choker necklace.

"Hi, I'm Sara. Are you new to the class?"

"Yes, actually. I'm Jules."

"I think we are sitting by each other. Here, follow me." According to the name cards, my desk was in the front, between Sara and a boy named William, whom I had yet to meet. I stuffed my backpack under my table—it barely fit, giving me very little room to put my feet. Before I could ask Sara any more questions, the school bell rang and everyone ran to their seats.

"Good morning, class! Welcome to your first day of school!" the young teacher called with a bubbly voice while walking to the front of the room. "My name is Mrs. Willis, and I will be your homeroom teacher. Now, as I call roll, I'm going to try to match some faces with some names here, so raise your hand when I call your name, all right?"

The teacher picked up a clipboard, taking a pencil from the front pocket on her pink floral shirt. I figured I would be near the middle of the list, since my last name began with an *O*. As Mrs. Willis called the names, I also tried to associate some names with faces. Minnie sat on the other side of the room a few rows behind me, between two boys who kept stealing glances at her face. There were twenty-one people in the class, and my name was seventeenth on the list.

"Well, children, it looks like everyone is here for the first day of school! So, to begin, I want to play a little game so we can get to know each other. When I call your name, you will walk to the front of the room and you will have one minute to tell the class what you think they should know about you. Then, once you finish, the class can ask you some questions," Mrs. Willis explained. "And since we have two new students in the room, I thought they should go first. In fact, y'all can go up together so it isn't quite as intimidating."

Oh, shoot, I thought as all eyes turned on me. *What am I going to say?* I jolted up out of my chair, tripping over the toe of my tennis shoe. Before I could even stand up and make my way to the center aisle, Minnie floated to the front of the room, her skirt flaring out as she spun to face the class. Once I managed to make my way to the front, she looked at me, tightening her red lips into a slight smile.

"Jules," Mrs. Willis called. "Why don't you go first."

"Oh, okay. Well. Hi, I'm Jules O'Connor. I just moved to Texas from New York City—"

"Oh, how fun!" Mrs. Willis interrupted. "Go on."

"I attended an all-girls school while I was there, so this is different for me," I joked, laughing weakly. No one else laughed. My hands started shaking so I held them behind my back. "Anyway . . ."

"Tell us your favorite place in New York," Mrs. Willis suggested, sensing my panic as I searched for what to say.

"I would have to say I loved just living in the city, being so close to the Broadway shows, all the museums, the various restaurants. But my favorite place in New York was definitely the Met . . ."

"What's the Met?" a boy asked from the back of the room.

"The Metropolitan Museum of Art. My school prided itself on being only one thousand steps from that museum, so we went there all the time."

"That is so fascinating, Jules," Mrs. Willis said when the class didn't respond. "Life in Texas must be very different for you."

"It is. I now live on a three-hundred-acre ranch with two horses, a pony, five dogs, a cat, and twenty-six longhorns. I can name all the longhorns too! Do you want to hear all their names?" I asked, getting excited about my new ranch skills.

The class was silent. My palms suddenly began to sweat as my legs started to tremble.

"Sure, honey," Mrs. Willis said uncertainly. "Do that for us."

"Well, first we have Old Respite and her daughter Clover, who has a daughter named Quaker's Prayer and a son named P.S. Quaker's Prayer has a daughter named Easter's Prayer—she was born around Easter. Old Respite has another daughter named Thymes Right, and she had a daughter named Valenthymes. Then there is Revolution— she is our prize cow with the longest horns—who has a daughter named Liberty, who had a son named Liberty's Snow. Revolution also had a daughter named Spangled Pride, who has three daughters: America's Pride, who is the mother of Star Pride, our newest addition; and her two other daughters, Spirit Pride and Sparkle Pride. Now, Revolution has a sister, Labor Daisy, who has never had a calf, and a sister named Fultz Flower, who is actually pregnant right now. And there's Tiger Bud, who will let me pet him like a dog. Then there is Bull's Eye—she got her name from the big bull's-eye on her side—who is the mother of Cotton Tail. Then there is Valentino, Bull's Eye's brother. Next there is Prairie Blossom's line. Prairie Blossom had Yellow Rose, who is the mother of Prairie Pewter. Prairie Blossom also had Prairie Prayer and Prairie Don Juan. How many is that?"

"That was twenty-six," Sara whispered. The rest of the class just sat in their seats staring at me, blinking every now and then.

"Well, my family has one thousand head of Angus cattle, but we just tag 'em and kick 'em out! Daddy told me never to name 'em. After all, they're for profit, not personal enjoyment," Minnie suddenly said, looking at me from the corner of her eye. Everyone turned their attention to Minnie.

"One thousand? Wow! That's a lot!" said one of the boys in the back of the room, looking at Minnie with big eyes.

"Nick, wait to speak until I call on you," Mrs. Willis said.

"It is a lot," Minnie replied in her melodious voice, stepping out in front of me, taking center stage. "I have a *five*-hundred-acre ranch in West Texas. Daddy takes me there with him all the time. When I go down there, I like to ride my award-winning palomino cutting horse. Daddy said I learned to ride before I could walk."

"Oh, I have a palomino too," I interjected. No one seemed to hear. Everyone's attention was still on Minnie.

"Often, when I'm down there, Daddy and I hunt deer and quail—"

"You hunt?" a boy shouted from the front row.

"I do!"

"That's so cool!"

"Girls," Mrs. Willis interjected, hoping to contain the class, "why don't you tell us your favorite verse of Scripture."

I froze. *Favorite verse of Scripture? I don't have any Bible verses memorized.*

Minnie answered first. "Well, Daddy always reads the Bible with me, Mama, and my sister Mary Louise over breakfast every morning."

I quickly scanned the walls for a Bible verse. *There has to be a verse on the walls here somewhere.*

Meanwhile, Minnie had no problem responding. "I've read so much Scripture, it is hard to really pick a favorite, but I must say, whenever I am feeling lost or afraid, I think of Mark 10:14. 'Let the little children come to me, and do not hinder them, for the kingdom of heaven belongs to such as these.' Daddy tells me to always think of that verse and of Jesus's love for me when I am feeling troubled."

"It's so wonderful to hear that your father is such a great example for you," Mrs. Willis said. "After all, the Bible tells us that the fathers are to be the heads of the households."

"Oh yes, ma'am, and Daddy certainly is."

"Jules, what is your favorite Bible verse?"

I was quiet for a moment. I scanned the room one final time for any source of inspiration, and my eyes fell on a binder belonging to one of the girls in the front row. A sticker with *3:16* was pasted on the front.

I hoped for the best. "3:16," I said.

"Oh, John 3:16!" Mrs. Willis exclaimed. "Such a great Bible verse and the foundation of the whole Christian faith. Did your father also teach you that verse?"

"No, ma'am," I muttered. I wasn't quite sure what to say.

"All right, girls, that was great. I could ask y'all questions all day, but we have to get to the rest of the class. Let's give them both a round of applause!"

I scurried over to my seat and sat down. Minnie, meanwhile, was still standing at the front, doing a little curtsy as the class applauded. Several of the boys whooped.

"You did great," Sara whispered. I smiled. The boy on my left sat quietly, twirling his pencil around his desk— his perfectly styled brown hair reminded me of Liam Hemsworth's.

Once she finished curtsying, Minnie glided past my desk, holding her head proudly in the air. The boy sitting beside me turned around as she walked by, staring at her as she walked to her seat.

"Okay, children, who wants to go next?"

"I think I need to brush up on my Bible verses," I moaned as I climbed into the car.

"What?" Mom asked, her smile turning into a concerned expression. "We read the Bible together."

"And I also need to invest in a curling iron and makeup."

"You're in sixth grade. You don't need to wear makeup," Mom said.

"Well, Minnie wears makeup."

"Who's Minnie?"

Where do I begin? "A girl in my class."

"Just because she wears makeup doesn't mean you have to," Mom retorted. "Are you a trendsetter or a trend follower?"

I sighed. "A trend follower."

There was a silence in the car. "What was your favorite part of the day?" Mom asked.

I thought for a very long time. "I recited all the longhorns' names and listed off every single pet on our ranch," I said.

"You did?" Mom smiled from ear to ear.

I nodded.

"What did everyone think?"

"I'm really not sure."

"I'm sure they loved it."

Silence once again filled the car—but this time I could tell there was something Mom wanted to tell me.

"What's wrong?" I asked her.

"So, I've been with Maggie all day and she isn't getting any better. I soaked her hoof in the Epsom salts, but it didn't help. I think I'm going to call another vet to get a second opinion."

"That sounds like a good plan," I replied solemnly. "Do we know another vet, though?"

"I called Kelly—you know, my friend who's a horse trainer in Kentucky—and she recommended someone. I gave him a call and he said he would come over when we get home."

"What's his name?"

"Dr. Peterson. Kelly said he just moved here from Kentucky and he worked on a lot of her horses."

"Well, we will hope for the best," I said, looking out the window, watching pastures filled with black cows fly by the car. Soon we passed Sammer's place—he had a tractor in his front pasture with a For Sale sign and fifteen baby cows grazing around his house. *Cows sure are nice lawn mowers, always eating the grass evenly.*

As our front gate appeared in the distance, I saw a shiny white truck idling on the shoulder of the road in front of our mailbox. Heat waves radiated from the hood of the truck.

"Looks like Dr. Peterson beat us here," I said. Mom rolled down the window as we approached. A young man, about thirty years old, sat in the truck, looking down at a phone he held in his hands. He had dark black hair and olive-colored skin. *I wonder if he is Italian.*

"Hi there," Mom said.

"Emily?"

"Yes."

"Hi, I'm Dr. Peterson."

"Howdy. I hope you haven't been waiting a long time. I just picked Jules up from school."

Dr. Peterson peered into the car past Mom and looked at me. He nodded and flashed a wide, white smile.

"No, not at all. I just got here actually."

"All right, follow us to the barn."

His white pickup followed us up the dusty gravel road, past the large oak tree, past our house where all four dogs yapped from behind the fence, all the way to the little blue barn. I heard R2's piercing whinny as we approached.

"So where is the mare?" Dr. Peterson asked, hopping out of his vehicle. His spurs clinked on the gravel as he made his way to the barn. As he walked by me, I noticed his towering height and strong build.

"She's right over here," Mom said. Maggie nickered from her stall. I immediately grabbed a handful of sugar cubes for her from the feed room. As we approached

Maggie's stall, I saw her standing in front of her stall door, looking out her window. Her left leg was relaxed so no pressure was on her hoof.

"Will you walk her for me?" Dr. Peterson asked, looking into Maggie's stall. Maggie lowered her head into her halter and then followed Mom out. Maggie's limp was still obvious. When Mom tried to turn her around to face Dr. Peterson, she struggled to keep her balance.

"This is definitely founder," Dr. Peterson said. "You can just let her stand still now. I want to look at her hoof just to make sure."

I rushed over to Maggie's side and delivered her the handful of sugar. She nibbled gratefully. Her eyes, however, seemed to lack their normal spunk and spirit. Meanwhile, Dr. Peterson bent down and rested Maggie's hoof on his knee, scraping the mud from around her sole. He pressed his hands around her hoof and inspected her sole. Maggie jerked her hoof away and dangled it above the ground. The vet sighed and looked at me and then at Mom with a concerned look in his eyes.

"I brought the clinic's portable X-ray machine with me as a precautionary notion, in case I found her in this bad a shape—"

"This bad a shape?" Mom gasped.

"This is a severe founder, and I don't want to mess around with it. Could I X-ray her hoof? It will tell me how much her hoof has rotated. I'll have to inject dye into a vein in her leg, which will tell me how much blood circulation remains in the hoof. I can have all of the results before I leave," Dr. Peterson explained. Mom rubbed her forehead with the back of her hand.

"Okay, do whatever you need to do," Mom said.

Dr. Peterson exited the barn and rummaged around in the trunk of his pickup.

"He seems like a very good vet," I told Mom. She nodded.

"I can't believe this. Poor Maggie," Mom said, hugging her mare. Maggie sighed, her nostrils trembling, as she turned and embraced Mom with her neck. Maggie then looked over at me and closed her eyes.

"All right," Dr. Peterson said. "Ready for an X-ray, Maggie?" He carried in an odd-looking machine and placed it next to Maggie's left hoof. It reminded me of something from the starship *Enterprise* from *Star Trek*: a thirteen-inch LED screen connected to a robotic arm that adjusted itself around Maggie's hoof as Dr. Peterson pressed buttons on the touchscreen. A long IV tube draped around his neck, leading toward a large bag of purple dye tucked under his arm.

"I'm going to inject this dye into the vein in her leg—it should give us all the information we need to make an accurate diagnosis," Dr. Peterson explained again. He knelt down next to Maggie's hoof, gently injected the needle, and squeezed in the dye. I looked away, feeling slightly queasy. I waited for Maggie to turn purple, but she didn't; rather, she stayed completely golden.

"Now she just has to let her hoof rest on this small platform here in front of the machine. I'm worried she isn't going to want to put a lot of pressure on it, though," Dr. Peterson said, rolling up the sleeves of his white button-down shirt.

It took a lot of time and coaxing to get Maggie to leave her hoof on the platform. Every time she applied pressure to her hoof, she immediately lifted it back up. One moment her hoof was on the platform, the next it was up in the air. Several times she kicked over the X-ray machine, sending wires flying into the air. I could have sworn I saw a twinkle of mischief flash across Maggie's eyes. Finally, she let her hoof down onto the box and left it there. We all cheered. The commotion caused Maggie to jump and lift up her foot and stomp it onto the ground, disrupting the whole contraption once again. This time Dr. Peterson caught the machine, wiping the sweat from his brow.

"That was good, Maggie. Do that one more time and we will take the pictures and be through, okay?" Mom cooed. Obeying the command, Maggie placed her hoof on the platform and left it there. This time, we were all quiet as mice. Dr. Peterson slowly walked over to the machine and clicked a button twice.

"Got it!" he exclaimed. Mom hugged Maggie on the neck and told her what a good girl she was, kissing her on the nose. Dr. Peterson smiled. "I'll go start loading this onto the computer in my car. Maggie can go back in her stall now." Mom slowly walked Maggie. She shook her mane, obviously grateful the whole ordeal was over.

While we waited for Dr. Peterson to return with the diagnosis, I hurried to clean the three stalls while Mom fed. Maggie, as usual, acted like she was starving, nose-diving into her trough once Mom dispensed her rolled oats and Equine Senior.

"Okay, if you'll follow me out to my truck, I can show you the results," Dr. Peterson shouted from the end of the barn. I clamored out of R2's stall, throwing the pitchfork into the wheelbarrow behind me, not wanting to miss anything.

The covered truck bed also looked like a modern technology phenomenon. The whole inside of the compartment was illuminated with light blue lights, and dozens of transparent drawers lined all three sides. Horse medication, shots, bandages, and even horseshoes were all neatly separated into their compartments. What really caught my attention, however, was the large laptop computer in the center displaying several different windows of X-ray results.

"The results aren't good at all," Dr. Peterson began. "You can see in this image here that there are only four millimeters of sole left between the coffin bone—that's her hoof bone—and the sole wall. That is an *incredibly* small amount of sole, and that is what is causing all of her pain. If you look above the bone here, you can see the inflammation that is pushing down on the bone. But what is even more concerning"—Dr. Peterson paused and pulled up another photo—"is the blood circulation test. As you can see, the base of her sole has no blood circulation anymore. That means that the hoof won't be able to regenerate any more sole. Essentially, her entire hoof is now dead."

I had no idea what the images meant. Dr. Peterson's words entered my mind like a foreign language, all jumbled and meaningless. All I could tell, from the look on Dr. Peterson's face, was this diagnosis was not promising.

"Oh no. Oh no. Oh no," Mom repeated, tears filling up her eyes. "It's all that farrier's fault. It's that farrier's fault."

After a pause, Dr. Peterson said, "There are very limited things we could do. I would say that Maggie has one month, maximum."

"Until what?" I asked, looking up at Mom.

"Hold on, Jules." Mom placed her hand on my shoulder, struggling to keep her voice steady as tears rolled down her face.

"If you wanted to try something," Dr. Peterson continued, "you could try shoeing her with different shoes in order to situate her feet at a different angle. That would lessen the tension in the tendon that is causing the rotation. There is also an option where . . ." Dr. Peterson trailed off. Mom had her face hidden in her hands and was breathing unevenly. I felt a wet droplet fall on my shoulder. My own breathing began to quicken—I even began to feel my lunch reenter my throat. What did this all mean? Surely this was fixable. To me, it all sounded like a broken bone that just needed to be reset. For some reason, neither Dr. Peterson nor Mom thought it would be that easy.

Dr. Peterson, increasingly unsure of what to do, looked around nervously before patting Mom on the shoulder twice. "Um, well, there is another option. Maggie can have a surgery where we go in and cut her tendon. It will immediately relieve the pressure on the bone and stop the bone rotation. The rehabilitation process is long and she would have to stay at the clinic for at least three months. Some of the horses are unable to stand up for the first month and have to eat and drink lying down. The outcomes aren't certain, but if it works, it will help."

"Maggie has never been away from the ranch since she moved here, and her spirit is too independent and free to be able to stand being paralyzed for two weeks," Mom said. "I think that will be too traumatic for her."

"The process is very traumatic, and I appreciate your reasoning on that. I'm not a strong proponent of the procedure," Dr. Peterson said. "I want you to try new shoes, though, and this new medicine." He handed over a bottle of huge white pills. I took them in my hands and inspected them. "Those are for pain and inflammation. Here is a name of a farrier I recommend for the shoeing. Call me when you have a date with the farrier and I'll come out to help in any way I can."

"Thank you, Dr. Peterson. You've been wonderful," Mom said.

"I'm so sorry I can't be of more help," Dr. Peterson said. "Call me if anything changes."

Dr. Peterson waved and stepped into his truck. As we watched Dr. Peterson's truck roar away from the barn, we were completely silent. Mom and I turned and walked back into the barn. Everything was completely silent. All I could hear was the whirl of the overhead fans. Even the cicadas seemed to have stopped chirping.

"Maggie is going to be okay, right, Mom?"

"I don't know."

"But . . . she has to be okay."

Mom didn't answer.

I ran forward, throwing open Maggie's stall.

"Maggie," I cried. Overcome with fear and sadness, I felt my eyes spurt tears as I began to sob. "Maggie, you can't do this. You just can't!" I fell to my knees beside her. She looked down at me, placing her nose onto my shoulder. I once again felt her warm breath against my skin, the scent of grass and carrots filling the air. Such sadness now filled her eyes. It felt like just a day had passed since I had chased her through her pasture, her spirit so alive and free. Yet that was now over a month ago.

Maggie moved her nose to my face, rubbing the tears from my cheeks with her nose. "That tickles, Maggie," I whispered, laughing through the tears. I stood up and kissed her on the face. Looking out through the stall, I saw Mom still standing in the middle of the barn, her face covered in tears as she pressed the back of her hand up to her mouth, attempting to quell the flow of emotions.

We walked back up to the house without a word, the air stagnant, not a sign of movement or life anywhere. My snake boots shuffled against the gravel, as my legs felt too weak to move. Gazing up to the sky, I saw only blue—not a cloud appeared for miles and miles; the sky was vacant. Seeing such vast emptiness made me feel small and inconsequential in the scope of everything around me. Powerless. Powerless to control nature. Powerless to change the track of life. Powerless to do anything to help Maggie.

Looking over at Mom, I saw her walking in silence beside me, staring blankly out into the horizon. I desperately wanted to say something, anything, to comfort her. But there was nothing to say and nothing to do. Sensing my gaze, Mom took my hand. Her hand was shaking slightly.

Even the dogs were quiet that day. All four of them sat on the porch, not even responding as we walked through the gate. Mom sat down on one of the wrought-iron chairs, her face glowing with the sunset. Our porch faced west, and as I looked out, I was amazed at how much farther south the sun now set. When we had arrived at the ranch three months earlier, the sun was far off to the northwest; now it set almost due west. As I looked toward the horizon, two scissortail birds chased each other over the road, hopping from tree branch to tree branch and then down to the pipe-and-cable fence. They darted through the air, spreading out their forked tails, turning in circles and loops.

"Jules, look," Mom whispered. She pointed to the road. Shading my eyes from the sun, I could see a cow walking on the road in front of the house.

"That's weird . . . Fultz Flower is never in the lead," I said.

"I don't see the rest of the herd. I wonder if—"

"Mom, look! She just gave birth."

A little baby trailed behind Fultz Flower. Fultz Flower proudly traipsed toward us, swinging her head from side to side as she looked for the rest of the herd. The little baby moved its tiny hooves at extraordinary speed, repeatedly tripping over its gangly legs as it tried to keep up with its speedy mother. The baby's black-and-white body was still covered in a milky film.

"This is the first calf to be born while we've lived here, and we get to witness it," Mom said. Although we had many baby longhorns, all of them had been born before we arrived.

"Why is she all by herself?" I asked.

"Well, longhorns go off into the woods by themselves to give birth and then bring their baby to the rest of the herd."

"Is it a boy or a girl?"

"I think it's a boy," Mom said. "We don't have many boys in the herd." The little bull swung his tail back and forth, twitching his ears at the sound of our voices. Upon seeing us, he stopped for a moment and belted out a pathetic moo before running back to his mother.

"Look, Fultz Flower hasn't lost her placenta yet." Mom pointed to Fultz Flower as she walked away from us.

"Her what?"

"You see what's hanging under her tail? That's what the little baby was in before it was born. That means she probably just gave birth a matter of hours ago."

Fultz Flower suddenly stopped, sniffing the ground to try to find a scent of the rest of the herd. The baby, who was too busy looking around at the new world, didn't see that she had stopped and rammed right into her back legs. He flopped to the ground, shaking his head.

"What should we name him?" Mom asked.

"Well, he's the first longhorn born since we moved back; it should be something about Texas."

"What about Tex?" Mom asked. "You know, that was Grandpa's nickname during his years at West Point Military Academy."

"I like that name, Tex," I said. "Let's see if he likes it. Hi, Tex!" I shouted to the longhorn pair. Tex twitched his little ear to acknowledge his new, human name and looked over his shoulder.

"I think he likes it," I said confidently.

"Now we have another baby to keep up with."

Little Tex. He would have to learn to fend for himself in the wild world of ranch life. I wasn't really worried about him, though; he seemed tough to me.

By the time we finished dinner, night was setting in, the moon rising above the house. I decided to sit down at my piano, which had, for so many weeks, remained untouched in the corner of the living room. Memories of playing the piano in New York City flooded my mind—I learned Bach's Prelude in C minor and played it in Steinway Hall on Rachmaninoff's ancient piano for my piano recital.

I had just begun to play when Chubbs came over and pushed her nose underneath my arm, causing my fingers to slip off of the keys. She once again carried her metal dog food bowl.

"Chubbs, come on, I'm trying to play the piano," I said. As I leaned over to give her a bear hug, I sniffed the top of her head. It smelled like horse manure.

I'm definitely in Texas, I thought as the moon streamed through the window above. The night was a solid-black stage curtain and the moon was the one spotlight that illuminated the stage. The world was so quiet.

I closed my eyes and began to play the piano again, imagining myself in Carnegie Hall playing with a symphony. Then I opened my eyes and realized that my Carnegie Hall was splat in the middle of no-man's-land. That was all right with me.

Culture in the country. That's not a bad combo.

seven

Waking up at six thirty in the morning was not my favorite thing to do on a Monday. But what other choice did I have when I lived forty-five minutes away from school? Then, of course, I had to add in the time it took to feed the horses, give the cows their morning water, make sure the dogs were situated in their doghouses in the backyard, etc.

Therefore, at six thirty, before the sun had even risen above the horizon, my alarm clock blared into my ear, rudely awakening me from a good dream and sending me out of bed. Fighting back yawns, I walked across my room, slammed on the light, and got ready for school. That consisted of getting on my uniform, quickly splashing some water on my face, brushing my teeth, then promptly going outside and putting General and Buster in the backyard, Chubbs inside, and Jessie on the front porch. We now had to separate the dogs in this way because Jessie had decided to start picking fights with Chubbs, General recently attacked Jessie, and Buster had started growling at everyone but General. *One big happy family.*

By the time I got back inside—with Chubbs at my heels carrying her dog bowl—Mom was already making our breakfast. While I prepared medicine for Jessie—a bronchial dilator for her recently developed asthma, Cortisone, and Lasix inside a spoonful of cat food—I saw that my morning breakfast consisted of an "Instant Breakfast" milk shake. *Okay. It could be worse.*

"Morning, Mom," I said, still very sleepy.

"Good morning," Mom replied. It was obvious that she hadn't gotten enough sleep either. Leaving the cat-food-filled spoon on the counter for a moment, I took a quick look at Mom's "Room Mom Roster" to see if anyone's birthday was today.

During the parent orientation two weeks before, Mom had signed up as room mom. The room mom's job was to decorate a child's desk when it was his or her birthday at school, organize all the class parties, etc. What Mom *hadn't* known was that no one else would sign up for room mom. Here we were, forty-five minutes away from school, and Mom was in charge of being to school fifteen minutes before the bell whenever someone in my class had a birthday. Of course, we were rarely at school fifteen minutes before class. Taking a quick glance at Mom's birthday chart, I saw a crisis fall right into my lap. *Oh dearest me.*

"Mom!" I yelled with a little bit of panic in my voice.

"What?" Mom said, whirling around and spilling little drops of milk all over the floor.

"Today is Minnie's birthday! Of all people!" Mom looked at the clock and turned a little bit pale. We were already running fifteen minutes *behind* schedule. I blamed General, who had refused to stand up until I had given him a full belly rub.

I knew this drill. I quickly grabbed everything we needed that morning and ran to the car. Mom's purse, her briefcase, my backpack, my lunch box, and the medicine kit—in case I had an asthma attack—all flew around me as I sprinted. After splashing through the mud created by our sprinkler and getting it all over my freshly cleaned white kneesocks due to our lack of a sidewalk, I got to the gate that led out of our yard.

Oh no, not today. The gate appeared jammed. After a lot of pulling, groaning, and body slamming, it opened. I dashed to the car. The car was locked.

"Great!" I yelled. I ran back to the gate, the bags still draped over my arms. The dogs started barking frantically. They obviously felt my angst. I took a quick glance around into the dark forest just in case they were warning me of an intruder—they weren't.

"Hush, hush," I whispered, trying in vain to get them to be quiet. General apparently wanted out of the backyard, so he decided to jump on the gate (which used to have a nice coat of white paint but had long since been covered in mud), succeeding in splashing mud on my nice white shirt.

"Now that's just wonderful," I said, giving General a glare. It was hard to stay mad for long while watching his bright pink tongue drip drool all over Buster's head. I quickly gave them all a pat on the head and sprinted to the door. Mom looked extremely puzzled as to why I was so out of breath.

"The car is locked," I stated. After swinging off my snake boots at the door, I grabbed the keys along with Jessie's spoonful of medication off the counter and ran back outside. Mom looked curiously at my mud-splattered shirt.

"General," I said. Mom turned back to making toast. I exited the house and found Jessie peacefully asleep on her bed on the front porch. "Wake up!" I whispered, patting her on the head. Jessie started and sniffed the air, sensing cat food was near. "Hurry, Jessie, I'm running out of time." After what felt like hours of coaxing, Jessie, who thrashed her head like a petulant child, swallowed her medication. I stood up, thanked her for her cooperation, and dashed to deposit all of the bags in the car.

I then decided to address my mud-covered shirt. This consisted of sprinting to my room and searching my uniform drawer, which meant throwing all my extra skirts into a pile on my bed.

"Aha!" I said, pulling out a wonderfully wrinkled white polo. After changing, I walked back outside, finding Mom already sitting in the car. That meant I now had to lock the door. As I slammed the door closed, the keys flew from my hand, wedging themselves into the wooden panels of the porch floor. I dropped to my knees to pick them up. When I yanked on the car key, Mom's presidential keychain popped open, causing all of her keys to scatter everywhere.

Not now. Not now. I scrambled to put all the keys back onto the keychain. Finally, I locked the door. Almost stepping out of the gate, I saw none other than Tiger Bud, the one longhorn who is not afraid of anything I do, eats out of my hand, and pretty much thinks he's a dog (granted, a mighty big, orange dog with horns). Mom had made me swear I would never go outside the gate if a longhorn was anywhere near. Thus, I concluded I must shoo Tiger Bud away from the gate. The question was, how? I did the first thing that popped into my mind.

"Shoo, shoo, ruff, ruff!" I tried desperately to scare Tiger Bud away, flailing my arms around. He was not frightened—rather, he stared at me with a bright, amused look. Then I thought of the one thing he loves: cattle cubes. I walked down to the opposite end of our yard and called Tiger Bud.

"Come here, Tiger Buddy, he's such a good boy, come here! I have a cube for you, come here, good boy," I said in my best coaxing voice, pretending to hold a cube over the fence. He seemed to move in double slow motion toward my outstretched hand. The moment he extended his tongue to lick my hand with his slobbery and rough tongue, I sprinted with all I had in me to the gate. I looked back to see where he was. He looked so confused and innocent that I *almost* felt sorry for him . . . but not quite. I rushed to the car.

"What in the world has taken you *so* long?" Mom asked. I pointed to Tiger Bud. Before she had time to respond, I realized I had left my gym bag in my closet. Once again splashing through the sprinkler-system-created mud, I ran back to my room, trailing mud the whole way, and grabbed my gym bag. *I really hope I have my gym outfit in there.*

As I approached the car for a fourth time, Mom poked her head out the window and asked, "Do the dogs have water?" I had no idea. I dropped my gym bag—straight into a clump of mud—and ran to the backyard. I waltzed by General and Buster, protecting my clean shirt from the two jumping dogs who really wanted my attention. Looking in their dog bowl on the back porch, I found it completely empty.

I don't have time for this, I thought, as the water flowed at an extremely slow pace out of the outdoor faucet. I impatiently watched the hands on my hot-pink watch tick away precious seconds of time. Once the bowl was full, I ran out of the backyard and through the gate. Swinging my gym bag into the back of the car, I managed to get mud all over my shirt for the second time that day.

"I am not changing again. I just don't have time!" I said to myself. Sitting down was a surreal feeling. As Mom drove down the gravel road to the barn, I sipped some of my breakfast and observed the weather. Overcast. Not my favorite weather condition. The early-September leaves looked hot and tired. The grass swayed as if to say good morning. It felt like yesterday was the start of summer, and at that moment I wished it was.

The car skidded up the hill and came to a halt right in front of the blue barn. We walked into the barn and were greeted warmly by the horses. Mom and I quickly wished them a good morning back and entered the feed room. I scooped up R2's half scoop of oats, grabbed her Cushing's medication to help lower her thyroid hormone levels that had peaked due to the heat, and hurried to her stall.

"Good morning, sweet R2," I said. She responded with the pinned-eared expression of "Yeah, yeah, just give me my food." I pressed my finger onto her squishy tongue, forcing her to open her mouth—getting horse slobber all over my hand in the process—and squirted the oral medication into her mouth. I then poured her oats into the little green bucket on the ground in front of her. I shut her stall and turned to deliver R2's, Rocky's, and Maggie's hay. I gave R2 her hay first, knowing she would get even moodier if I didn't. I then gathered Maggie's hay.

"Good morning, Maggie! How do you feel today?" She was already occupied with the oats Mom had given her.

Maggie's left leg was wrapped in bandages—Dr. Peterson's latest idea—but she still lifted it up off the ground repeatedly, as if her bedding had turned into hot coals. I sighed. "Hang in there, Maggie."

Next, I picked up Rocky's hay and entered his stall with my arms overflowing. Rocky seemed unusually cranky this morning. I put down his hay in his bucket and then turned to leave.

Isn't it strange how your mind knows what is about to happen before you're aware of it? After throwing down the hay, everything seemed to decelerate into slow motion. All I remember is that I felt this excruciating pain in my . . . let's just say very lower back, and fell to the ground, catching a glimpse of the horrific image of Rocky staring at me with his teeth bared. Then everything zoomed back into normal time. Rocky ran out of his stall, leaving me in a tangled heap in his hay. I must have hit the ground for only one second, though, as I was back up again before Rocky was totally out of his stall. I then realized that Rocky had successfully bitten my "lower back" through four layers of clothing: a school jacket, skirt, shorts, and underpants.

I must have screamed, because when I ran out of the stall crying, Mom was already by my side. I was in so much pain. It felt like someone had shot me *and* stabbed me with a knife in my . . . very, very lower back. Mom locked up the horses' stalls, told them all a brief "Love you," and then led me to the car. We drove back up the gravel road and Mom pulled into the driveway.

"No, d-don't stop-p, we have-have to get-t to sch-school to d-decorate Minnie's desk-k," I stuttered in between sobs and coughs.

"We will, but we have to doctor you up first," Mom coaxed. I saw a look of worry in her eye. I knew what she was thinking.

"Mom, Rocky-y got his-s rabies shots-s already-y," I said, gulping for air. *Why on earth would Rocky bite me?*

"Boy oh boy," Mom said, trying to erase the look from her eyes. I stayed in the car, watching the clock in anguish—partly because of the pain but mostly because of the time—while Mom dashed inside to get the antibiotic ointment and the hydrogen peroxide to "doctor me up." What I really needed, however, was to alleviate the pressure of sitting on my . . . lower back.

Mom came back outside with the ointment, hydrogen peroxide, and a lot of Band-Aids. I gritted my teeth as Mom poured the stinging liquid onto my wound. I was thoroughly *not* enjoying the experience of having my . . . lower back doctored in front of a herd of staring cows. Finally, after Mom stuck eight Band-Aids over the bite, we hopped back into the car and sped down the driveway. The cows leisurely chewed their cud in the dewy grass, not having a care in the world. I wondered what it was like not to be on any schedule. *It must be rather peaceful.*

"Why did the car stop?" I asked Mom, wondering if we had run out of gas.

"Look, look, look!" Mom cried, pointing to the road in front of us. I winced as I tried to sit up. Outside the window, a large feline ran across the gravel road into the forest.

"I think that was a bobcat!" Mom said. I suddenly wondered if I had closed the gate to the yard thoroughly. I hoped the dogs wouldn't get attacked by the bobcat.

Yet the bobcat quickly disappeared, and I wondered when Mom was going to take her foot off the brake. Finally, Mom began to drive to the gate again and we were on our way.

The car ride to school was horrible. For one, I had to sit on the bite wound the whole time. Then Mom called the veterinarian's office asking if they had ever heard of a horse contracting rabies even after it received its rabies shots.

"Well, it's rare . . . Have seen once . . . rare," I heard the receptionist saying over the phone in a garbled voice.

Wonderful! Not only do I have to be in pain all day, I have to worry about whether I might get rabies. I rolled my eyes and plopped my head in my hands.

When we finally got to school, we were fifteen minutes late. That means thirty minutes later than when we needed to arrive in order to decorate Minnie's desk. I suddenly felt sick at the thought of Minnie and how she thought she was Miss Popular. One thing about Minnie was that she was always complaining about how the basketball had broken her hot-pink fingernail in gym, or how her blonde hair hadn't curled the way she wanted it to. You never dared to compliment her either. One time a boy had been "mean" by saying her hair looked nice instead of beautiful. I knew one thing right away: when Mom walked inside and stood on Minnie's desk in her muddy clogs full of horse bedding in order to tie some balloons on the ceiling, Minnie would not be happy.

"Hey, Mom, since class has already started, don't you think you should decorate Minnie's desk at lunch?" I asked in my most innocent voice. Mom thought about that for a moment as we walked down the hallway.

"How about I ask Mrs. Willis if I would be interrupting the class if I did it right now?" Mom asked me in return.

"Okay." I sighed and looked at the floor. I walked into class, sure my eyes were beyond puffy from crying and that all those Band-Aids on my . . . lower back were making a huge bulge. Mom and I were quite a pair. She wore a black, pink-striped jogging suit that was about two sizes too big for her, along with muddy clogs and a brown hat she'd purchased in Ireland that covered her "bad hair day." Mom walked over to talk to Mrs. Willis while I situated all my books at my desk.

"Sure! We just started our vocabulary exercises," I heard Mrs. Willis say. Mrs. Willis was so sweet, she wouldn't have said no to Mom even if she had been in the middle of teaching the class about the Battle of the Bulge. I realized that I might as well just enjoy the look of terror on Minnie's face when mud, hay, and horse bedding fell out of Mom's shoes and onto her desk. I winced as I plopped into my chair, forgetting to sit down slowly.

"Excuse me, Minnie. Would you mind if I decorated your desk for your birthday?" Mom asked from behind me. I turned around.

"Oh, not at all, Ms. O'Connor!" Minnie said in her polite, countrified voice that just impressed the breath out of adults. "Go right ahead," she added with a sly look of disgust at her new best friend, Tina, who sat in the back of the room giggling. Mom stood on Minnie's desk and hung up the pathetic pink-and-purple balloons I'd filled up on the drive to school with our portable handheld balloon pump.

Standing on her tiptoes, attempting to reach the ceiling, Mom almost lost her balance. I quickly dropped my pencil onto my desk and held Mom's one free hand to prevent her from plummeting to her embarrassment. When Mom stood to lodge the tattered balloon strings into the ceiling panels, out fell all the bedding and mud from her shoe, just as I expected. The class gasped and whispered, "Eww," to one another.

"Mrs. Willis! Oh, Lordy me! Get Ms. O'Connor off my desk, *now*! Ugh," Minnie yelled, stomping her foot and purposefully sitting on the chair Mom was just about to step onto to get down. Mom tilted precariously far off the desk, looking as if she was about to jump for it. I quickly grabbed my chair for a stool and she stepped down. The class started to giggle. I couldn't tell if it was at Mom or Minnie or both.

Mom gave me a kiss, grabbed her old orange purse, said her good-byes to Mrs. Willis, and started to walk out. I looked at Minnie, who had gone to her desk but now refused to sit down until the bedding and mud were swept from her desk. She refused to touch any of it herself, and stood with her nose turned up and arms tightly crossed. Therefore, I walked over to Minnie's desk, swept off all the mud and hay into my hands like her servant, and neatly threw it all into the trash, secretly wishing my nature was not so sweet. Mom still stood in the doorway, so I gave her a look of "I told you so" and "Don't worry, that's just Minnie." I returned to my seat, sitting down slowly this time.

"Where were you this morning?" my now best friend, Sara, asked, leaning over from her desk beside me.

"It's a long story," I replied. "I'll tell you later." I risked a glance back at Minnie, who chatted furiously to Tina, turning quite red. I knew they were talking about Mom. *I wish they would stop.*

Mrs. Willis was still talking to Mom outside the classroom. I then realized I had forgotten to give Minnie the official class birthday goody bag, which I had also frantically put together in the car that morning. I walked to my book bag and located the goody bag. Finding it slightly crumpled, I tried desperately to straighten it out. I peeked inside the bag to see what I had thrown in there: a purple bouncy ball, a blue beaded bracelet, and a roll of bird stickers.

Just then, I realized the horrible mistake I'd made; Minnie detested purple. I walked very slowly over to Minnie's desk.

"Hey, Minnie, I forgot to give you this," I said, smiling.

"I wondered," Minnie said while giving me an "I'm better than you" look. That hurt more than my . . . lower back. I sat down in my chair. Sara noticed my spirits changed.

"What's wrong?" she asked. I waved my hand because I couldn't talk.

"Purple! Ugh. I hate purple," I heard Minnie exclaim right behind me. I then got up for the second time, this time quite resentfully, and dug into the cluttered pocket of my book bag in an attempt to find the pink bouncy ball I had received in my birthday goody bag earlier that week. I knew that Minnie loved pink like all the rest of the girls in my class . . . except Laura, who was a tomboy and would never admit to liking pink. I faced Minnie again.

"Would you like a pink one instead?" I asked Minnie, avoiding eye contact. She didn't even look back at me—just held out her hand and continued her obviously "very important" conversation with Tina. I hesitantly gave it to her. She plopped the bouncy ball into the bag and left the purple one in there as well. I didn't dare ask her for it either.

"Class, attention, please. Now that everyone is here, please get ready for the reading of the lunch menu," Mrs. Willis said as I sat back down. "Today Jules will be student of the day," Mrs. Willis chirped, looking at me.

Please, no! Any other day but today! I slowly got up and shot an uncomfortable glance at Sara.

"Um . . . today's lunch is fruit salad and fried chicken with creamed corn. Ice cream is the dessert," I said, summing up the lunch menu. I wanted to be up there for as short a time as possible.

"What's the sandwich?" Harry shouted. The one thing I had forgotten to read. I turned back around to read the end of the lunch menu, knowing perfectly well Harry was not interested in the sandwich and was instead interested in giving me a hard time.

"Peanut butter and jelly," I said. My voice was giving and my vision was blurring. It had been a crazy, hectic morning. I wouldn't be caught crying in front of the class, though, especially in front of Minnie.

"Are there any prayer requests?" I asked while grabbing a pencil. Four people raised their hands. I called on Harry first to get him out of the way. He always seemed to hate me and I had no clue why.

"For my dog. It just had puppies."

All the girls cooed.

"Congratulations," I said.

"Whatever," Harry replied.

"Susana." I called on one of the sweet, quiet girls for a relief.

"For my mom. She caught a cold over the weekend."

"I'm sorry about that," I replied slowly while writing all this down.

"Fredrick."

"For Minnie's birthday to go well," Fredrick said, winking at Minnie.

"Fredrick, how sweet, you shouldn't have!" Minnie said in her thick southern accent. I rolled my eyes to myself.

"For Minnie's birthday to go well" I wrote. The pencil tip broke. I took a fresh one from the pencil jar on the table.

"Sara."

"For my cat, it's sick."

"With what?" I asked, extremely curious if I could assist in any way.

"We don't know. It's at the vet's right now."

"Is that all?" I asked after I took a few more requests. No one else raised their hand. "We're ready," I told Mrs. Willis.

"All right, class, let's pray."

While Mrs. Willis opened the prayer, I looked down and in horror saw that I had forgotten to change my knee-socks. They were almost brown with mud.

"Jules?" Mrs. Willis whispered to me, startling me out of my personal inspection. I realized it was time for me to read the prayer requests.

"Oh," I started. "Dear Lord, I pray for Harry's dog, who just had puppies; I pray that you heal Susana's mom from her cold, and for Sara's cat; and . . . for Minnie's birthday . . . to go well. Amen." I rushed through the prayer and turned to go back to my seat.

"Hey, Jules! What's that in your hair?" Nick, Harry's twin, taunted. I stroked the back of my head. My hand bumped into a long, pointy object that felt longer than my own hair. As I touched it, dry green leaves fell to the floor.

Oh dear. I'm in for it now. I gingerly removed the hay stick from my frizzy hair, succeeding only in sending another avalanche of green leaves and small sticks onto my shoulders.

"I don't know what you are talking about!" I said in my innocent and cheerful voice.

"It was green and looked like *hay*!" Harry chimed in. I don't remember what happened next, but I'm sure I turned beet red.

"How was your day?" Mom asked when I clambered into the car after school.

"Um . . . Well, I made a one hundred on my history test." I tried to start with the best thing in my day.

"That's wonderful!" Mom said, being a typical mom.

"Yeah, but not the part of my day when Harry and Nick discovered the piece of hay in my hair! Sara had to go with me to the bathroom and help extract the thousands of dry alfalfa leaves stuck in my thick hair. And we still didn't get them all out!" I said in a desperate tone.

"Oh dear."

"Yeah, and Minnie ended up with *two* bouncy balls, because I forgot that she hated purple with an earthly passion and so I gave up my pink bouncy ball, thinking that she would trade it out, but *no*. She decided to keep both of them. Plus, I was student of the day today with mud all over my kneesocks!" I pointed to the disgraceful socks. I was really on a roll.

"It's okay," Mom said, stroking the back of my head. "Do you want to listen to some music?" On the drive home we listened to 95.3 FM "The Range," which was playing "All My Exes Live in Texas," and sang so hard, I knew the surrounding cars could hear us. That cheered me up. When we got to the ranch, I hopped out of the car to open the old gate and waited for Mom to drive through. Once the dust cleared, I latched the gate behind me and climbed back into the car. We parked in front of the house.

"Don't we still have to feed?" I asked Mom, puzzled. We usually always drove up to the barn on school days.

"Yeah, but I thought we would walk and enjoy this day," Mom said, eyes fixated on the blue sky.

We decided not to take the dogs because they always ran off, and it was getting late. The dogs were very upset with that decision. The cows were pleasantly grazing around the house and didn't notice us walking up. I was sure we were pretty noticeable, though, given Mom was in the bright yellow, oversized Donna Karan windbreaker she had owned for ten years, which reached the ground and made her look like a banana. I was rather unsure as to why Mom was wearing such a jacket on this hot day.

The moment we opened the large, rickety barn door, Revolution gave out her long, distinct moo that we knew meant, "I am ready for my cubes and you're not leaving without giving me some." I sensed we were up a creek now: no car, no refuge.

We tried to feed the horses and muck the stalls in record time, trying to beat our old record of five minutes. Mom instructed me to start dissolving one of Maggie's horse pills in a syringe, so I ran to the feed room, filled the syringe with hot water, and plopped in one of the enormous horse pills. As I shook it back and forth, little droplets of medicine flew all over my uniform. *Wonderful.*

"Here, Maggie," I said, walking into her stall. Mom stood beside her already. I decided to let Mom give her the medicine. Maggie, however, was not very cooperative. She backed up out of Mom's reach and tossed her head back and forth, jerking to the side the moment the syringe touched her mouth. She clamped her mouth down so tightly that Mom couldn't get the syringe inside. By the time Mom finally managed to squeeze the chalky medicine onto Maggie's tongue, half of it had spewed across Mom's face.

"Phew!" Mom sighed. "You have never been a good medicine taker, Maggie."

Revolution mooed in the distance.

"Mom, we should go."

"I'll be back after dinner, Maggie."

We left the barn ten minutes after we arrived. By that time, some of the cows surrounded the front of the barn, which meant that exit was now blocked. The only exit left to us now was to walk through Rocky's pasture, where the gate at the end opened up to the road. Mom and I were almost to the gate when I realized we were in more trouble than we originally thought. Valentino, the de facto leader, stood on the road to our left; Labor Daisy, Valentino's right-hand woman, stood in front of us, blocking the closest gate entrance to our yard; and last but not least, Revolution stood on the right, staring at us fervently with fire coming from her nose as she kicked dust into the air.

"We can make it—let's go," I said, trying to sound as brave as possible. All three longhorns watched our every move.

"I'm not so sure," Mom said.

"Come on," I said, climbing through the gate. That was when Mom and I learned rule number one: never listen to my advice when your life is on the line, especially when it includes cows.

As I exited onto the road, Valentino, Labor Daisy, and Revolution approached in a slow trot. Our pathway to the house was quickly narrowing. Valentino swung his horns, which looked thicker than my entire waist.

"Run!" Mom said.

We also learned rule number two: never run around longhorns. The moment we began to run, we had Revolution, Valentino, and Labor Daisy all loping toward us, thinking we had invited them to a footrace. Before I knew what was happening, I had a longhorn within ten feet of me on every side. I had never seen a longhorn eye so clearly before. Mom, out of mother's instinct, grabbed onto my arm, taking a little bit of my hair in her grasp in the process. With every stride, she pulled a handful of my hair. Boy, did it hurt. *One thing's for sure: a longhorn's horn going through my stomach would hurt a lot worse.* It must have looked comedic. Here we were—Mom in her big yellow raincoat, me with my head tilted to prevent half of my hair getting ripped out—running for our lives from our own longhorns, who were probably chuckling to themselves and thinking how incredibly slow and awkward looking we were.

When we were on the last leg of the run for our life—which happened to be the small, narrow passageway between our white picket fence and a forest of prickly vines—we had Revolution at our heels.

"Run, Jules, run!" Mom shouted, urging me to run ahead to safety. Somehow I managed to work myself free from Mom's death grip and sprint to the gate. When I did, I left Mom right in front of the big exposed tree root. Mom forgot to step over it and tripped. It was like a scene from a horror movie: life slowed down as Revolution approached, swinging her horns, running full speed, kicking up dust and rocks. She looked like a bull in a fighting ring, and Mom was the red flag. Mom worked to keep upright while hydroplaning and tilting closer and closer toward the dirt as Revolution galloped nearer. Right before she hit the ground, however, Mom miraculously managed to catch her balance and continue running. She made it to the gate one second after I unlocked it. Revolution then ran by the gate one millisecond after Mom and I flew safely through it. I latched the faulty latch shut and collapsed from exhaustion onto the first stepping-stone I saw. Mom struggled to catch her breath.

"I can't breathe, I can't breathe, my throat is dry, my throat is dry," she said, gasping for air in a little bit of a panic mode, walking around in circles like a jogger after a marathon. She coughed twice. "I think I'm in a-fib."

I think I'm in shock. I need a shock blanket. Revolution almost trampled us to death and we had just finished running the fastest five-hundred-meter dash of our lives. I wondered how and if we were still alive.

We managed to make it inside and drink some water.

"Aw, man! My zipper broke. This was my favorite raincoat," Mom said, shedding her banana suit. I couldn't help but laugh. Our meanest cow had just chased us at full speed, and the worst that came out of it was a broken zipper. In one day, Mom and I both experienced a narrow escape from our animals: me from Rocky when he bit my . . . lower back with a force I didn't know existed in him, and Mom from the wild, cube-addicted Revolution.

I don't think the word *sleep* ever sounded so good in my life.

Eight

Sunlight beamed through my curtains. For some reason, once again I was at the foot of my bed while Creampuff was sprawled all over my pillows. It amazed me how her small, fluffy white body managed to take up two pillows. *It's Creampuff's world.* Rolling over, I looked at my wristwatch and saw that it was eight thirty in the morning. I almost panicked, thinking I was incredibly late for school, but then realized that it was Labor Day. Enjoying the silence of my room, I flopped my head back onto my bed.

On the ranch, however, leisurely mornings did not exist—there were horses to feed and cows to count. I heard Grandpa's voice in my head saying, "Real cowgirls get up with the sun." I dutifully rolled out of bed. Walking across my small room, stepping over Buster who had fallen asleep at the foot of my bed, I flung open my curtains.

"Ah!" I screamed. I stared straight into Revolution's eyes, her face just inches from mine. I could even see the whites of her eyes and her long white eyelashes. Somehow Revolution had managed to get into the yard and was standing on the back porch, apparently waiting for me to awaken. "Didn't we just go through this, Revolution? I don't exactly have cubes right now."

Upon seeing Revolution at the window, Creampuff— not immune to the sight of longhorns—began ferociously barking at the window. *As if she really stands a chance next to a longhorn,* I thought, watching her white puffy tail wave back and forth. Revolution regally began to turn around. As she walked off the porch, she looked over her shoulder at me, as if warning me she would return. I gulped.

I turned and walked to the opposite side of my room and opened the other curtains, finding that the gate to the yard was wide open. Thankfully, Revolution swayed back through the gate to rejoin her herd.

"Jules," Mom asked, walking into my room, "are you awake?"

"Well, I just woke up. Revolution was on my back porch," I explained. *I swear that longhorn is stalking me.*

"How strange. I guess one of us left the gate open. That's Ranch 101, you know: always lock the gates behind you."

"I know that! I blame the finicky latch," I said, walking into my bathroom. No matter how hard I tried, the gate to our yard never stayed fastened.

"We need to go feed the horses, so make it snappy," Mom said through the door. "I have an egg sandwich on the table for you so we can eat as we walk."

"Got it!"

After throwing my hair into a ponytail and putting on my jeans and a tank top, I grabbed my breakfast sandwich off the kitchen table and joined Mom outside.

"The weather is so nice at this time of day," I said through a mouthful of sandwich. *Instead of 105 degrees, it's only 85.* Dragonflies darted around our yard, landing on the still-dewy grass. The sky was pleasant: wispy white clouds veiled the light blue sky, reminding me of a frosted cookie. Leaning against the fence, I took a moment to soak in the beautiful, serene nature. As I looked up at the sky, however, I saw a small object flying toward me—right toward me. To make matters even stranger, the thing seemed to be screaming, like an overflowing teakettle on a stove. *It must be some kind of insect.* My jaw dropped as the insect grew closer and closer, larger and larger, louder and louder, making a definitive beeline for my face. Before I could do anything about it, the insect—now the size of my palm and emitting a deafening screech—flew straight into my face. To be more precise, it flew straight into my mouth, landing on my tongue.

"Aahhh!" I yelled, flinging my egg sandwich into the air, gagging and trying to get the object out of my mouth. Spinning my hands all about my face, I ran around the yard, shaking my head, desperately trying to dislodge the insect from my mouth. I gagged even more and spit. The insect fell to my feet. *"Eww-w-w-w,"* I screamed with a shiver, dancing around and shaking my hands. I immediately closed my mouth, not wanting anything else to fly in, but refused to swallow. I felt like Lucy after Snoopy licked her mouth—except I just almost swallowed a Texas-sized bug.

Mom doubled over in laughter behind me. "What was that?"

I was afraid to open my mouth to respond. Instead, I tiptoed back over to the bug, which now lay dead in the grass. I assumed it had died from fright. The insect was the size of my palm and had wings longer than my thumb. *I don't know how that even fit in my mouth.*

Mom walked up behind me. "Oh, it was a cicada," she said.

"A really large cicada," I added. Eager to leave the yard, I began walking to the barn, clenching my jaw tightly, keeping a keen eye on my surroundings to prevent any additional collisions with gigantic bugs.

"Good morning!" I yelled at the top of my lungs upon entering the barn. R2 whinnied loudly. Rocky kicked his stall door gently, notifying us of his hungry belly. "I'm working on it . . . I'm working on it."

Picking up several sugar cubes from the feed room, I sneaked by Mom and delivered a sweet treat to Rocky. His eyes seemed to say "Thank you." Next, I decided to check on Maggie and also give her a sugar cube. Walking over to her stall, I called, "How's Magg—" but stopped midbreath. I dropped the sugar cube onto the floor, reaching to open her stall door. My heart skipped a beat and my throat began to constrict as I fumbled with the latch, my hands sweating.

"Jules, are you okay?" Mom asked from the feed room. Upon seeing how frantically I opened the stall door, she came running.

"Oh no!" Mom yelled. "Maggie, hold on!" She ran to get her phone from the white rocking chair.

Maggie was lying flat out in her stall, breathing heavily. I fell to my knees and landed next to Maggie's head. "Maggie, are you there? Are you okay, Maggie?" I asked, stroking her face. The palomino opened her eyes and lifted her head. She touched her nose to her hoof and snorted. "I know it hurts, Maggie. Do you want some Bute?" I looked over at the door. Mom's footsteps pounded through the barn. When she came into view, she was holding her phone tightly to her ear, and miraculously seemed to have reception.

"Kelly? Kelly, are you there? Hold on one second." Mom looked at me. "Jules, you talk to Kelly and bring some Bute paste to me. I'll stay with Maggie."

I scrambled to my feet and took the phone from Mom, who ran by me, falling to the ground, cooing to Maggie to try to comfort her. I looked back and saw Maggie nuzzle her nose into Mom's hand, then press her whole head into Mom's chest.

"Hello, hello?" I heard Kelly's voice come through the phone.

"Oh, Kelly? It's Jules," I said, walking to the end of the barn, hoping I wouldn't lose cell service.

"Hey, Jules, what's up? Is everything okay?"

"No. Not at all. We just walked into the barn, and I found Maggie flat out in her stall. It's not like she was sleeping or anything. It's eight forty-five in the morning and—"

"Jules—"

"Why would she be lying down? Is this normal? Do you think she was just resting or something? But if she is, why is she—"

"Jules, stop!"

"Yes?" I finally stopped my frantic mumbling. I realized I had been pacing the front of the barn and had forgotten all about the Bute. I ran into the feed room and flung open a cabinet, letting boxes of other medication fall onto the table below as I searched for the Bute. My hands were shaking.

"Jules, calm down for a second. Whatever you're doing, stop for a moment and listen," Kelly said, her voice calm. I hesitated with my hand in the air, reaching for the Bute on the second shelf of the cabinet. The phone was lodged between my shoulder and my ear, and my other hand clutched the table. "Now, can Maggie get up?"

"I don't know; she hasn't tried," I said.

"Jules?" Mom shouted. "I need that Bute *now*." I grabbed the Bute and ran to Maggie's stall. Maggie had her front feet pushed against the ground, sitting like a dog. She seemed to be trying to gather the strength to stand up.

"Kelly, it looks like she might try to stand up soon."

"Okay. Now, Jules, we need to know, first, if she can get up and, second, if she can stay standing," Kelly said.

"What happens if she can't?" I asked, hushing my voice. I walked over to sit in the rocking chair.

"Then this may be it," Kelly said.

"It? What do you mean *it*?" I exclaimed, tears starting to fill my eyes. My fingernails dug deep crevices in my palm as I rocked back and forth.

"If she is in too much pain to stand, it means her hoof bone has pushed through her sole wall, and there is nothing you can do for that. You can't get her in a trailer to get her to a vet clinic or anything."

I bit my lip. My eyes went to the floor, my chest rising and falling. I suddenly felt hot and flushed, as if my tank top had turned into a trench coat.

"Jules?" Kelly asked. "What's happening?"

I stood up and walked over to the stall. Maggie had one back leg underneath her and was trying to figure out the best way to approach getting up.

"She's still trying to get up," I said, wiping my face. I didn't want Maggie to see me crying.

"Good girl, Maggie, you can do it. Oh, oh, come on, Maggie," Mom coaxed. Maggie fixed her eyes on me as if asking me for strength.

You can do it, Maggie. I know you can do it.

Maggie popped her back legs under her and hopped up. She resituated her legs, wobbling a little.

"Good girl, Maggie! You did it!" Mom cried, hugging Maggie's neck in hopes that she would remain standing. "Hand me a sugar, Jules, to keep her mind off of her hoof."

"Jules, is she up?" Kelly asked.

I bent down to the ground and picked up the sugar cube I had dropped. "Yes, she is up. She seems pretty stable, but she hasn't tried to move yet." I handed Mom the sugar cube while walking farther into the stall to stand by Maggie. Maggie shook her head, her mane sending pieces of bedding through the morning air.

"All right then, Jules, hand the phone to your mother. I need to talk to her. Take care now."

I handed the phone to Mom, who cleared her eyes with the back of her hand. I saw her mouth quivering. She walked out of the stall and I heard her start to cry.

"Oh, Maggie," I sighed, leaning into her neck. We looked out of her stall window together. "Just a month and a half ago we were running around that pasture. What happened? Hmm? What happened?"

Maggie looked at me and lowered her head a little bit as if she felt she had let me down.

"I am so sorry, Maggie. I am *so* sorry. I would do anything to help you, girl," I said softly into her ear. She nudged me in the chest, sending me onto the floor. "Now look who's on the ground?" I laughed. She seemed to tell me all was well in her heart. Standing back up, I brushed the bedding from my jeans and kissed Maggie on the neck. We stood there for a while longer, looking out at the tall, billowing grasses of her pasture. She sighed, her nostrils trembling. Maggie had not one sign of age on her—that was the horrible thing about it. She was still in her prime, looking like she came right out of a picture book. Maggie's spirit inside still wanted to be free, but the sadness in her eyes revealed that she knew that was no longer a possibility.

"Jules?" Mom asked. She walked into the stall. "I called Dr. Peterson. He told me that it is time to try the shoes he talked about. He has a farrier who works at his clinic who specializes in founder treatment. Dr. Peterson assured me that this farrier has saved dozens of founder patients before. He wouldn't cut her back at all. All he would have to do is put these special shoes on. Dr. Peterson convinced the farrier to come in on Labor Day since this is an emergency situation."

I looked over at Maggie, who appeared to be listening to the conversation as well. *Mom and I will do anything to help you,* I told her.

"There's only one problem," Mom said with a long exhale.

"What?"

"The farrier has to work from the vet clinic, since some of the equipment he uses isn't portable, so we have to take Maggie to the clinic."

"But we don't have a pickup truck . . . or a horse trailer."

"I know."

I thought for a moment. One of Maggie's ears turned to the side. She obviously was not looking forward to going to the vet clinic.

"Sammer!" I yelled, startling Mom.

"What?"

"Sammer had a trailer and a pickup! Call him!"

Mom immediately left the stall to call Sammer.

"Hi there, Sammer, how are ya?" I heard Mom ask from the front of the barn.

"Well, it looks like we're going to a vet clinic," I told Maggie.

Within fifteen minutes, Sammer pulled up to the barn in his black pickup truck with the horse trailer hitched behind.

"Howdy!" he shouted, slamming his car door. His appearance shocked me: instead of his traditional overalls, alligator-skin cowboy boots, and a cowboy hat, he wore khaki shorts, a T-shirt, and tennis shoes—obviously his around-the-house outfit.

"Hi, Mr. Sammer," I called, walking up to him.

"Where's the mare?"

"Over here," Mom called from the stall. She already had Maggie haltered and began leading her slowly toward us. At the sight of the horse trailer, Maggie balked, refusing to budge from the center of the barn, reminding me of a toddler refusing to enter the doctor's office.

"Maggie, come on."

Maggie appeared to say no.

After much coaxing and persuading on Mom's end, and after much pulling and pushing, Maggie was loaded into the trailer and we were off to the clinic.

"That's it," Mom said, pointing to a small, red-roofed building connected to a large horse barn.

"I see it, Emily," Sammer said. Sammer was behind the wheel, and I sat in the backseat of the pickup, repeatedly looking over my shoulder to check on Maggie. Every time we hit a bump in the road, I worried that Maggie would lose her balance and fall. But from what I could tell, she looked perfectly fine. Though I could barely see her through the slats in the horse trailer, I caught glimpses of her golden coat shimmering in the sunlight, and every now and then I caught her eye and smiled.

"How's Maggie doing?" Mom asked, looking over the bench seat at me.

"She seems to be doing fine," I said.

As soon as Sammer threw the truck into park, Mom hopped out and ran to the horse trailer.

"How was your ride, Maggie?" Mom asked. I quickly joined her side. Besides looking windblown, Maggie seemed to be enjoying herself, her ears pricked forward and her eyes wide with excitement. *That's a good sign.*

"Hello, Emily," said Dr. Peterson, walking up to the truck. He greeted Sammer and then joined us at the back of the trailer. "We have to take her straight into the barn. The farrier is waiting for us in there."

Mom nodded and proceeded to lead Maggie gently out of the trailer. Maggie's metal shoes clopped loudly against the steel trailer, vibrating my eardrums at an unnaturally high frequency.

"There! That wasn't that bad," Mom said once Maggie was on the ground. Mom, however, was covered in sweat, and her blonde hair was slicked to her face. She handed the lead rope to Dr. Peterson, motioning him to guide the way.

"You can either follow us or wait in the lobby until—" Dr. Peterson started.

"We'll come with you," Mom said, immediately rejecting the notion of letting Maggie out of her sight.

"I'm gonna stay here with the truck," Sammer shouted.

"That's fine!" Mom replied. Maggie limped considerably as she walked before us, barely wanting to put any weight on her left hoof. As soon as we reached the stable doors, a large chorus of whinnies filled the air. The magnitude of the sound reminded me of the Hallelujah chorus from Handel's *Messiah*.

Maggie immediately perked up and began whinnying in response. Dr. Peterson laughed.

"What's so funny?" I asked him.

"She's talking with all the boys," he replied, looking at Maggie. Her eyes were bright as she nickered constantly. The stallions reared in their stalls and paced back and forth as Maggie's beautiful figure passed through the barn, her tail arching as she swished it glamorously through the air. She flung her mane as she passed the stalls, flaunting all of her beauty, reminding me of Cher from the movie *Clueless*. I figured Maggie was having a wonderful time talking with all of her adoring fans.

"Emily, this is Stetson Jones." Dr. Peterson introduced Mom to an elderly man who stooped over a pile of shoeing equipment.

"Hi, Emily, pleased to meet ya," Stetson said, extending his hand. His deep voice seemed to contradict his appearance: he stood at five-foot-six and had a slight build. He wore leather chaps over his blue jeans and a checkered shirt.

Mom shook his hand before motioning to me, saying, "This is my daughter, Jules."

Stetson tipped his hat before turning to Maggie.

"Before I begin, Emily, I want to show you the shoe," Stetson said, beckoning Mom over to his pile of equipment. He lifted up an object that I would hardly call a horseshoe. It looked more like the high-heel wedges Mom wore in the summer. In addition to the shoe, Stetson picked up a brown rubber pad that he would place over Maggie's sole.

". . . And when you put this on her foot, it turns the hoof in such a way that it will take the pressure off of the bone. It won't stop the rotation, but it will hopefully lessen the pain," Stetson concluded.

"How is she supposed to walk in this?" Mom asked, holding the shoe in her hand.

"Oh, she'll manage," Stetson said, bending down and beginning to remove the nails that held Maggie's current shoe to her hoof. "It might take a little getting used to, but she will."

Maggie looked over at me, seeming to ask me what in the world was about to happen.

"Look! There's Rocky standing outside in his pasture, waiting for Maggie!" Mom pointed as we pulled back up to the barn. Rocky stood at the far end of his pasture, looking expectantly at the road as we approached. Upon seeing the horse trailer, Rocky took off running, galloping beside us all the way back to the barn.

"Well, would you looky there. He's waitin' for his girl-friend to git back," Sammer said, trying to suppress a smile.

"It's true! Rocky has loved Maggie from the moment he saw her," Mom said, defending Rocky. "He was probably worried sick about where she was."

"Well, she's back now," Sammer said, turning off the ignition.

Mom immediately hopped out of the truck to check on Maggie and I quickly followed to help maneuver Maggie out of the trailer. She was now a substantial two inches taller, walking like a young girl trying to wear her mother's high-heeled platform shoes. Slowly placing one hoof in front of the other, Maggie made her way out of the trailer and onto the gravel road. Rocky immediately nickered, relieved to see his best friend alive and well. Maggie nickered back, flicking her tail. As Mom led Maggie into her stall, I checked her water supply and also brought her evening meal.

"You deserve your dinner after a long car ride, don't you?" I said, stroking her mane. She already stood in front of her little box fan, letting the breeze refresh her hot skin.

"Thanks again, Sammer, for coming to our rescue," Mom said while exiting Maggie's stall.

"Not a problem! Now I'm a-goin' fishin' for the next two weeks, so tell all them critters to stay out of trouble, 'cause I won't be able to come over here 'n' help save 'em," Sammer said.

"All right," Mom said, laughing, "I'll be sure and tell them."

"Where are you going fishing?" I asked.

"Oh, just over yonder in Louisiana. Cousin has a place over there, so I'll be stayin' with him."

"Well, have a good trip," Mom said, turning to go check on Maggie once again. I could tell she was still worried and very suspicious about the new shoes.

"Oh, I will! I'll be sure to bring over some of the fish I catch when I git back," Sammer added. "Y'all like catfish?"

I nodded. I didn't think it was the time to mention Mom was allergic.

"All right then, see y'all later!"

Sammer closed his truck door and revved the engine. Just as I turned to check on R2, who stood in her stall waiting for a treat, Sammer rolled down his window and shouted, "Hey, Jules!"

"Yes, sir?"

"I've got a bag of apples back here in my truck that I was gonna throw out. Do you wanna give 'em to your horses?"

So that's what was in that bag. I had seen a mysterious sack in the back of Sammer's car, but I had decided not to snoop around.

"Yeah, sure," I said. I walked out of the barn and over to his truck to receive a large, unwieldy sack of apples.

"There ain't nothin' wrong with 'em, I just don't like apples very much," Sammer said, seeing my curious expression.

"Well, thanks! I'm sure the horses will be very appreciative." I waved with my one free hand as Sammer drove away from the barn, the trailer clanking on the gravel road.

"What was that all about?" Mom asked, walking up to me.

"Mr. Sammer just gave me a bag of apples to give to the horses."

"We've never given them apples before."

"Really? Horses eat apples all the time in movies."

Rocky whinnied when I mentioned "movies." He stood at the end of his pasture near the far gate. I was always baffled as to why he stood there, since there was no shade in that area during the hottest part of the day.

"I'm sure you ate apples all the time during your showbiz days," I shouted, walking over to him. "I can give him one, right, Mom?"

"Well . . ." Mom slowly made her way over to us. "I don't see why not."

I placed the bag onto the ground and pulled out one large red apple. After inspecting it and wiping it off with my shirt, I extended it to Rocky. He looked at it, very confused at first about how to bite into it, and sniffed it with his huge nostrils, his nose whiskers tickling my fingers. Finally, he took a bite, consuming half of the apple.

"Look at that. Professional showbiz horse at his finest," I said, looking into Rocky's eyes. Mom and I watched as he chewed, sending apple juice all over his mouth. He smacked his lips up and down, apparently enjoying the treat. Pricking his ears forward, he extended his nose through the fence in an attempt to grab the rest from my hand.

"Not too fast, Rocky," Mom warned. Before I could pull back my hand, Rocky snatched the remaining apple with a large crunch.

"Well, there goes the apple."

As Rocky continued munching, I turned to look at the barn. Seeing the wheelbarrows parked on the side of the barn, I suddenly wondered where Bandana the cat had run off to—I hadn't seen him in a few weeks. *Those feral cats, so unpredictable.*

"What in the world?" Mom exclaimed. I turned back around and nearly collapsed. *You've got to be kidding me.* Rocky was slowly lowering himself to the ground. I suddenly began to doubt my trust in movies. *Maybe horses aren't supposed to eat apples.*

"Rocky, what are you doing?" I asked, completely dumbfounded as to why Rocky was standing before me eating an apple one moment and then splat-down on the ground the next.

Rocky also looked very bewildered at the situation, looking up at me in consternation as if he, too, was wondering how he ended up on the ground.

"For cryin' out loud," Mom cried. "What's wrong with *you*, Rocky?"

"Maybe I shouldn't have given him the apple," I whispered.

"You said horses ate apples all the time!"

"I thought they did."

Before I could place any more blame on the apple, however, Rocky started to roll.

"Oh, he just wants to roll." Mom sighed. "Geez Louise, Rocky, you gave me a heart attack."

But Mom spoke too soon. Rocky had overestimated his distance from the fence, so as he thrashed his legs in the air and rolled back toward the fence, his two back hooves collided with the cables. *Clink, clink, clink.*

Before he could do anything to stop it, both of Rocky's back legs poked through the cables, which prevented him from moving. He tried to roll again, but his back hooves hit the cables with a giant clank. Realizing he was now stuck, Rocky stayed still as a rock. Mom bent down and placed her hands on his legs to keep him calm.

"Here," Mom said, "help me push him backward."

I sat beside Mom and pushed on Rocky's back legs. No matter how hard we pushed and shoved and pulled and tugged, however, Rocky wouldn't budge.

"Come on, Jules," Mom said, straining. "Push!"

"I . . . am . . . pushing," I panted.

It was to no avail. To make matters worse, Rocky couldn't use his front legs to pull himself out, because his arthritis prevented him from bending them completely. He relied heavily on his back legs in order to stand up, but now they were trapped under the pipe-and-cable fence.

Rocky sighed.

"What do we do?" I asked.

Mom was silent for a moment before she shouted, "Call Sabrina!"

"Sabrina? Who is Sabrina?" I asked, wondering if my brain was on vacation.

"Our neighbor! She has horses, so she might have an idea," Mom explained. I wondered what "neighbor" meant in this situation. "I have her number on my phone. Go grab it from the barn and I'll stay here with Rocky to make sure he doesn't move."

As confused as I was, I ran back to the barn. Finding Mom's phone on the old stereo, I searched through her contacts until I found *Sabrina Rogers*. It beeped in my ear, telling me that the call had failed. So I darted out of the barn, running past Mom, yelling, "I have no service." When I reached the top of the hill, the call connected.

"Hello?"

"Hi, this is Emily O'Connor's daughter—"

"Hey there, Jules! How is it goin'?" I didn't know how she even knew my name.

"Um, well, my mom asked that I call you, because we have a problem."

"What's the matter?" Sabrina's tone of happiness fell.

"Rocky, our horse, managed to get his legs all caught up in our fence, and we can't move him out. We aren't sure what to do . . ."

"Tell your mother to hold on. I'll be right over in my golf cart."

"Thank you!" I said. I hung up the phone and walked back over to Mom.

"She is coming over right now in her golf cart," I said.

"It's okay, Rocky boy," Mom cooed. "It's all going to be okay. We will get you up."

We sat beside Rocky for what felt like fifteen minutes, the late-afternoon sun pelting down on us. Unfortunately, the one tree in Rocky's pasture had died, so it cast absolutely no shade. I felt like C-3PO standing on top of the sand dunes on the planet Tatooine in the Star Wars movies.

If Sabrina doesn't get here soon, Rocky's going to turn into a deep-fried chicken wing and I'll be the broiled potato on the side. Just as I was about to give up hope, I heard a golf cart squeaking up the gravel road. Behind the wheel sat a petite woman in her midfifties with dirty blonde hair pulled back into a ponytail.

"Hey, Sabrina," Mom said.

"Hey there, Emily! How ya doing? Well, don't answer that," Sabrina said, assessing the situation.

"His two back hooves are caught here under the cable, and his knees won't bend because of his arthritis," Mom explained. "Jules and I couldn't push him back, either."

"Well, if that is the case, then it is an easy fix," Sabrina said. I wondered what made her say that. "Got a rope?"

Assuming that was my cue, I ran to the barn and unhooked Rocky's halter from his stall door. R2 whinnied, wondering why in the world she still had not received her treat.

"Right here," I panted upon returning to the scene.

"What we have to do is this: turn him around so he faces away from the fence. That way, as he gets up, his legs won't get stuck."

"How are we going to do that, though?" Mom asked. I remained quiet, hoping this rescue effort wouldn't involve a great deal of engineering or fence cutting.

"We have to tie his back feet with this rope here—so he won't thrash around—and then rotate him around by pullin' on the rope."

I felt a disaster looming. I slowly backed up and sat down on a large lump of sand. Sabrina expertly tied Rocky's back legs together and handed the rope to Mom, who was looking quite pale. Sabrina moved to Rocky's front legs, which she gathered in her hands. Rocky looked very concerned as to why he was taking on the appearance of a wild boar before it's roasted over a fire. But before he could move a muscle, Sabrina held Rocky's front legs in place while Mom rotated Rocky ninety degrees by pulling his back legs. Slowly but surely, Rocky was freed and the rope was taken off his back feet. He hopped up, hoping to avoid any more leg tying and body rotating. Mom now looked unusually red and Sabrina wiped sweat from her face.

"See, wasn't that easy?" Sabrina asked. Mom didn't answer.

"Thank you, Sabrina. Sorry to call you on such short notice like that," Mom said, still panting.

"Hey, it ain't a problem," Sabrina said. "I'd stay and chat, but my grandsons are at the house and—"

"Oh, of course! Go, go, go. Sorry to have interrupted your family time."

"No, no, no, don't you worry about it. That's what neighbors are for! Just be sure to come over for dinner sometime. You know where to find me."

Southern people are so nice.

"We sure will," Mom answered.

"I'm gonna hit the road. See y'all soon!" Sabrina shouted, sliding into her golf cart.

Mom and I waved as Sabrina's little vehicle jumped up and down over the gravel road.

"So where does she live, again?" I asked.

"She lives about ten miles down the road."

"Okay. Good to know."

"Let's go check on Maggie," Mom said, a look of worry reentering her eyes.

We walked back down to the barn, finding Maggie standing by her window. I wondered how long she had been watching all the commotion.

"How's it going, Maggie?" I asked. Mom leaned over and kissed Maggie between her ears. Maggie nickered.

"You look like you can stand pretty well in your new shoes," Mom said. Maggie bent her head to the floor and sniffed her shoes. She seemed uncertain.

Suddenly, she lifted her head and looked intently out of her window.

"What is it?" I asked. Following her gaze, I could see the longhorns moseying toward the barn from the distance. "Hey, Mom, the cows are coming up."

"Oh boy. That means we're stuck here for a while." Neither of us was planning to walk through a hungry herd of longhorns again anytime soon.

Despite their constant grazing, the herd reached the barn in remarkable time. Mom and I moved to the front of the barn to watch them pass and count them to make sure they were all present and accounted for.

"Look at little Star Pride!" Mom clucked. Star Pride clopped by the barn, trotting after her mother, America's Pride. Star Pride was the cutest little calf in my opinion: a solid roan color except for a white lightning bolt on her back leg and the snow-white tip of her tail. Additionally, she was born into the lineage of our prize cows: Revolution had a daughter named Spangled Pride, who gave birth to three daughters—America's Pride, who was five; Spirit Pride, who was three; and Sparkle Pride, who was the same age as Star Pride. I collectively called the clan "the Prides."

Right as little Star Pride walked in front of the barn, Prairie Blossom came out of nowhere and pushed Star Pride away from her mother. Now, Prairie Blossom was pregnant, due to give birth any day, and probably felt very left out since she was one of the only cows in the herd who did not have a baby in tow. So instead of waiting to have her own, it looked like Prairie Blossom intended to adopt Star Pride temporarily. This was a big mistake. Star

Pride looked very confused as Prairie Blossom continued to push her farther and farther away from her mother. The whole herd stopped to watch. Star Pride bleated like a goat, sending America's Pride spiraling around to defend her daughter. Upon seeing Prairie Blossom ushering her baby away from her, America's Pride let out a long moo. Star Pride mooed back. Prairie Blossom did not respond, hoping to steal Star Pride without detection. As if.

Suddenly, America's Pride charged Prairie Blossom, butting her head into her rear end. Prairie Blossom turned around and locked horns with America's Pride, their horns clicking as they pushed each other back and forth in a longhorn version of tug-of-war. Star Pride stood to the side, looking completely lost and afraid.

"Oh no!" Mom yelled. "Stop, America's Pride! Prairie Blossom! Whe-e-e-e-w!" Usually the cube call immediately stopped any fighting, yet America's Pride and Prairie Blossom continued sparring. America's Pride gained ground, pushing Prairie Blossom away with her horns, but then Prairie Blossom twisted her head and hooked her horns under America's Pride's chest to send her stumbling backward. It reminded me of watching two lions duke it out at the Central Park Zoo. The other cows, on the other hand, began to moo, now wanting their cubes from Mom.

Before I could say anything on the matter, Spangled Pride, America's Pride's mother, emerged from the forest on the other side of the road like Robin Hood and charged toward Prairie Blossom. Spirit Pride and Sparkle Pride followed behind her, the threesome looking like the Three Musketeers running to save the day.

"Mom, look, it's the Prides!"

Sending her daughter to safety, Spangled Pride body-slammed Prairie Blossom and then locked horns with her. *Momma bear mentality at its finest.* America's Pride ran over to Star Pride, who still looked completely dazed. It was now three against one for Prairie Blossom, and she knew it. I could tell she was trying to back out of the situation—maybe even apologize in longhorn language—but Spangled Pride did not permit it. Spangled Pride began shoving Prairie Blossom backward on the gravel road, dust nearly obscuring them from our sight.

Mom began using the cow call nonstop, sounding like a broken record, as if we really could do anything to control two fifteen-hundred-pound animals who were deadlocked in a fight. Poor Prairie Blossom continued skidding backward on the road, desperately trying to dislodge her horns from Spangled Pride's, but to no avail. Spirit Pride and Sparkle Pride followed, as if urging Spangled Pride along. Mom and I watched in disbelief as Prairie Blossom was pushed backward half a mile: away from the barn, past the horse pastures, all the way past the arena, and into the forest.

"Oh no! The creek is back there!" I exclaimed.

"Oh, not again," Mom said. She ran into the barn and swung onto the four-wheeler, reminding me of Woody mounting Bullseye in *Toy Story*. I hopped on behind her, not wanting to miss the action. Mom revved the engine and drove behind the arena. We arrived just as Spangled Pride emerged from the forest, puffing her chest, proud of a job well done . . . but without Prairie Blossom.

"Prairie Blossom!" I called. Mom drove the four-wheeler through the opening in the trees that led to the other side of the creek. "I don't see her," I told Mom.

We retraced our path and searched behind the arena once more. "Oh, there she is," Mom said. I peered into the forest and saw Prairie Blossom standing there, looking exhausted and exiled but relatively unscathed.

I laughed at her astonished expression. "She won't try that again!"

"Yeah. Talk about mommas coming to their daughters' rescue! And America's Pride is five years old!" Mom said.

"I seriously thought Spangled Pride was going to run Prairie Blossom over the creek bank," I said. "I'm very glad she didn't, because I don't think Sammer would have been able to lift Prairie Blossom out with one hand."

I couldn't help but marvel at the strength of the mother-daughter bond among the longhorns. Spangled Pride had come to her daughter's rescue, nearly risking her own life defending her family. I looked over my shoulder to see Spangled Pride walking back over to check on America's Pride, who was licking little Star Pride on the head.

I looked at Mom, who sat in front of me on the four-wheeler, and hugged her a little tighter.

Nine

Big rain clouds loomed on the distant horizon, reflecting the morning sun. Additionally, some smaller, rapidly moving clouds carpeted the sky overhead, making the temperature a welcome ten degrees cooler. Unfortunately, however, the humidity level was through the roof. This was the first break in the monotonous cycle of hot, dry days and it appeared I was about to experience my first Texas storm. Thunder rolled in the distance. The birds didn't seem to mind the weather, though: beautiful robins hopped around the front yard, pecking at grass that brushed their red breasts, and phoebes darted through the air, chirping their staccato calls. The air was filled with the hum of cicadas and crickets. In addition to the peaceful sounds of nature, I heard a tapping noise coming from the driveway. Turning my head to inspect the origin of the sound, I saw a red cardinal hovering around Mom's car, incessantly pecking at the side mirrors, thinking its reflection was another bird.

A strong, stormy gust of wind slashed through my hair, cooling my neck. *Boy, that felt refreshing.* Such a leisurely Saturday morning was greatly appreciated after a long, stressful week—a week of six-thirty mornings, late nights studying for tests, and the continued stress regarding Maggie, who still made no improvements. In fact, she was getting worse. The day before, she had refused to touch her breakfast—ominous behavior from a horse who always nose-dived into her food. For dinner, she had only eaten a handful of oats out of my hand. Mom even tried pureeing carrots and sugar for her, but Maggie still refused everything. Instead, I found acorn kernels in her teeth—very disturbing, since acorns could be toxic for horses.

"Oh, you're awake!" I heard Mom's voice behind me as she appeared in the doorway. Before she could exit onto the porch, Chubbs, General, Jessie, and Buster all pushed their way through the door, desperate to relieve themselves in our yard, almost knocking Mom off her feet.

"Good morning," I said, stretching my arms.

"What are you doing out here?"

"I woke up at about six o'clock with a nightmare, so I decided to watch the ranch awaken in order to get my mind off of it."

She didn't ask what my nightmare was about. She knew better than to inquire.

"Look, I think we might finally get some rain," I said.

Mom sighed. "That would be nice, wouldn't it?"

I nodded.

"Hey, Jules, I want to hurry down to the barn to check on Maggie."

"Me too. I just have to put on my snake boots."

After donning my proper ranch attire, I walked outside and joined Mom, who already stood at the end of the porch, staring out into the horizon.

"Ready?" I asked.

"Yep."

Country music blared from the old, rusty stereo as we approached the barn.

"Good morning!" I exclaimed to the horses. Instead of the normal chorus of whinnies, there was only silence. Mom immediately turned the radio down. Rocky, who usually looked at us expectantly for his food, had his head lowered to the ground, seeming to sniff the shavings. I exchanged a look with Mom. Before I could say anything, she ran to Maggie's stall.

"Oh, Maggie!" Mom cried. My snake boots thudded against the concrete as I ran to Mom's side. Mom bent over Maggie, who was sprawled in the middle of her stall, covered in wetness.

I stood at the stall door but couldn't make myself go in. I turned around but couldn't lift my feet. I wanted to escape, hoping that if I ran away Maggie's pain would cease to exist—but I was paralyzed. My hearing went out as the world spun around me, and I remembered my nightmare. I broke down into sobs.

"Juliette, stop, stop, don't let her hear you cry." Mom looked me in the eyes and I tried to choke back my tears. *I have to be strong for her.* I steadied my frantic breathing and bit my lip.

"I'm going to go get the pain medication for her. Sit here with her and keep talking to get her mind off of the pain." She ran to the feed room.

I still stood in the middle of the barn. The sight of Maggie's open stall door sent shooting pains down my arms and hands. Silent tears streamed down my face. I looked over at Mom, and she motioned me to go into the stall. Somehow, I entered.

Maggie's whole body trembled, her breathing labored. Upon sensing my presence, Maggie looked and tried to lift her head, but it fell back down. She tried to nicker, but nothing came out.

"Oh, Maggie," I moaned, no longer able to combat the torrent of emotions that tore through my body. "Don't go, Maggie. You can't leave me!" I leaned my head onto her elegant neck. She nudged my knee. I realized in that moment that Maggie needed me; she needed to know I was going to be okay. "It's okay, Maggie. I'll be okay. I love you, Maggie girl. You're such a good girl, you know that, right? My sweet Maggie May." For a moment, Maggie lifted her head, her body becoming still. She placed her whole head in my lap before weakly letting it slide back onto the floor of her stall. Her whole body once again began to tremble. I looked away. I couldn't take Maggie's sweet spirit tortured by so much pain.

Mom returned to the stall carrying a tube of medicine. "Help me hold her head," Mom said. I lifted Maggie's head and Mom squirted the medicine onto her tongue. Maggie didn't even try to swallow. I lowered her head back onto the floor.

"I have to go call the vet now." Mom ran out of the stall. Soon I heard her talking on the phone to Dr. Peterson.

"It's okay, Maggie. Shh, it's okay." I bent down and kissed her forehead. Her eyes were dull, vacant, masked in pain and fear.

Mom ran back over and kneeled beside me. "The vet's coming," she whispered to me. Maggie, upon seeing Mom, perked up and pulled on the last reserves of her energy to hold her head up longer. She looked at Mom with such loyalty and love, desperately wanting to please her beloved owner.

In her frenzy, Maggie decided to stand up, trying one last time—for us. Thrashing around in the bedding, Maggie struggled to her feet in her high-heeled shoes, sending Mom and me rushing out of her way. Her body quivered so that she could hardly keep her balance. She looked around anxiously, confused, not knowing what to do or how to stop the pain. She tried to walk forward to Mom, pressing her head into Mom's hands, her teeth grinding so strongly I saw the muscles in her jaw. Maggie then turned and dunked her nose in the water trough. But she did not drink. Her nose dripping, she looked at me for guidance. I didn't know whether to encourage her to move or stay standing. So I remained quiet. As her eyes locked with mine, I could see her frantic determination not to let us down. She tried to walk to me, but it was too much. Her legs buckled under her and she tilted to the floor, landing on the bedding.

"Maggie! No! Don't fall!" I screamed. "Maggie!" I fell down next to her. My ability to speak abandoned me as my throat constricted with emotion. I could hardly breathe.

Mom fell beside me, whispering to Maggie. Although tears lined her face and her forehead contorted with pain, she kept her voice steady as she talked. "Maggie May, my sweet, sweet palomino. You've been my buddy for eighteen years. Eighteen years! Can you believe that, Maggie? You've been my best friend. My *best* friend." Maggie moved her neck so that her nose touched Mom's knee.

A car rumbled down the gravel road, gray dust filling the air. The vet had arrived.

"No!" I cried, stumbling over to Maggie's stall window. Dr. Peterson was getting out of his truck. "Tell him not to come in. Tell him not to come!" I yelled, running back over to Maggie and covering her head and neck with my body, trying to shield her from the inevitable. Maggie's coat still smelled sweet.

"He has to, sweetheart; she is in too much pain. He has to," Mom said, holding both of her hands in front her mouth, trying to hide her emotions. "Come here."

I ran to her and buried my face in her chest.

I couldn't believe that this was the last moment I was going to have with Maggie. The last moment I was ever going to see her beautiful face. The last moment I would ever connect with her magnificent spirit. I looked down at her, lying helplessly at my feet. She was looking at me. Through my tears, I could tell she was trying so hard to stay with us.

"Maggie, you are the best horse in this whole world," I shouted, my eyes blurring with tears. I looked away. Mom pulled me with her out of the stall.

"Hello?" I heard the vet call.

"We are back here," Mom said.

The vet met us in front of Maggie's stall.

"Is it time?" Mom asked quietly.

"She's done. Look at her eyes," Dr. Peterson said.

"No, Dr. Peterson, no! You can't take Maggie away!" I sobbed.

"Jules." Dr. Peterson knelt in front of me. "Look over at Maggie."

I looked into the stall. Maggie still quivered.

"Do you really want her to stay like that?"

I shook my head no. I didn't want her to be in any pain.

"I hate putting horses down more than anything. But I have to tell myself that I am taking them out of their pain, releasing their spirit from their agony."

I couldn't speak. Dr. Peterson stood up and walked into Maggie's stall.

"Wait!" Mom yelled. "I have to pray over her." Still holding on to me, Mom walked back into the stall and knelt by Maggie's head. "Our Father, who art in heaven, hallowed be thy name. Thy kingdom come, thy will be done, on earth as it is in heaven. Give us this day our daily bread, and forgive us our trespasses, as we forgive those who trespass against us. Lead us not into temptation, but deliver us from evil. For thine is the kingdom, the power, and the glory forever. Amen."

Dr. Peterson stood behind us with his hat under his arm. Mom looked up at him.

"I have to take Jules out," Mom whispered. Dr. Peterson nodded and we walked by him toward the other side of the barn.

"I love you so much, Maggie!" Mom shouted, her voice breaking. "Remember that, okay? I love you so much. You're such a good girl!" Maggie lifted her head at the sound of Mom's voice and let out her beautiful, deep-throated nicker, her eyes becoming clear and bright one last time. She seemed to tell us, "I love you."

She dropped her head back down and closed her eyes.

I turned my face into Mom's chest and hid myself in her arms. Mom's chest shook as she held me, and I felt her tears fall onto my head. Everything became quiet. Not a bird chirped, not a bug hummed, not a breath was taken. The whole world seemed to stop.

Suddenly, a strong gust of wind blew through the barn, moving the white rocking chair, blowing hay into the air, and slamming the stall doors against the barn. R2 whinnied at the top of her lungs. I looked out: she stood in her pasture, looking up at the sky. I realized at that moment that Maggie was gone from this earth forever. I collapsed onto the barn floor and sat, hugging my knees.

Dr. Peterson walked back out from Maggie's stall, wiping his eyes. "Where is her halter?" he asked.

"Hanging on her stall door," Mom replied. "Why do you need it?"

"For her burial. It is a Native American tradition that you bury the horse in their halter and face them west, toward the sunset. It is so they can be led to heaven."

I felt dull inside. Looking out through the barn windows, I saw a large tractor pulling up dirt and grass at the end of Maggie's pasture. I looked away. Maggie's stall was now desolate. No beautiful palomino standing in front of her fan, her hair blowing back like a model on a magazine cover. Never again would she take a sugar cube from my hand. *I wish I had given her one last sugar cube, letting her leave with that sweet taste in her mouth.*

Rocky stood at his stall door. I wondered what he was thinking, how he was feeling. Did he know Maggie was gone? Yes, he knew. His head lowered to the ground.

Resting my chin on my knee, I closed my eyes. They stung when I closed them. My hands gripped the sides of my legs until I was sure my knuckles were turning white. But I couldn't feel any physical pain. *Where is Maggie? Surely she's in heaven.* I looked up to see a little brown-and-white bird entering the barn, twittering up to the top of the barn ceiling. Flying from one side of the barn to the other, it landed right on Maggie's feed trough, warbling a beautiful call. I'd never seen that bird before.

"Jules?" Sammer stood at the front of the barn. I assumed he had been the one on the tractor, digging Maggie's grave. He took his hat from his head and walked over to me. I stood up from my puddle of tears. "I sure am sorry about your mare. But she's properly buried now in that pasture of hers."

"Thank you," I croaked, trying to fathom my beautiful Maggie now deep under the ground. Mom walked slowly to my side.

"Thank you, Sammer." Mom's voice was gravelly, her face weak, and her shoulders slumping.

"Do you need anything before I go, Emily?" Dr. Peterson asked. I had forgotten he was still in the barn.

"No," Mom said. "Thank you, though."

"Mornin', Dr. Peterson," Sammer said solemnly as the vet exited the barn. Dr. Peterson nodded and then left in his truck.

Silence filled the barn as the roar of Dr. Peterson's truck faded into the distance. The wind settled down for a moment, leaving a still, breathless silence.

"Nothin's worse than losin' a pet," Sammer said with a sigh. "And she was such a perty one."

"She was, wasn't she?" Mom wiped her face with the back of her hand, her mouth trembling.

I turned my head at the sound of another car approaching. "Mimi's here?" I muttered to myself. I looked at the white Mercedes that drove to the front of the barn and parked. Behind the wheel, I saw my grandmother, wearing her burgundy sunglasses and her favorite leopard top. Grandpa sat in the passenger seat, wearing an Alaska sweatshirt, his white hair crumpled under a baseball cap.

"Look who's here. It's Maurice and Lorraine," Sammer said.

As I started putting the pieces together in my brain, I realized that when Mom had called Dr. Peterson, she had also called Sammer and Mimi.

Mimi opened the car door and traipsed into the barn, tiptoeing around the dirt. Grandpa struggled to get out of the car, slamming the door behind him.

Mom ran over to Grandpa and hid her face in his shoulder. Grandpa didn't say a word. He understood. He always had a strong attachment to pets like we did.

"Well, hello there," Mimi said upon seeing Sammer in the center of the barn.

"Howdy, Lorraine. Good to see you, and good to see you too, Maurice, but sorry it's such sad conditions. Emily, if ya need anythin', just give me a holler."

"Thanks, Sammer."

Sammer walked out of the barn, heading back toward the tractor. Meanwhile, Mimi walked over to me and gave me a hug. Much to my surprise, she was drying her eyes.

"Now, we just have to stop having these bad days," she said with a choked laugh. I managed a half smile before diverting my eyes again to the ground. Grandpa walked over to a stack of shaving bags by Rocky's stall and sat down. Seeing that I was staring at him, he beckoned me over, placing me on his knee. He kissed me on the forehead, his scruffy beard tickling my skin.

He understood that words were meaningless at a time like this. The silence was welcoming. I just leaned my head against his shoulder. His sweatshirt smelled like cat and dog hair mixed with cologne.

Mom stood alone, leaning against Maggie's stall door, looking down at the place where Maggie had last lain.

"Emily?" someone asked from the front of the barn. I turned to look over Grandpa's shoulder and saw two people standing in the barn's threshold: Sabrina and Mason.

"Sammer called me and told me about your mare," Sabrina said. "I'm so sorry. I lost my mare last spring. Puttin' her down was the hardest thing I've ever done."

"Oh, Sabrina," Mom said, walking over to our neighbors. "Thank you for stopping by." I slid off Grandpa's lap and joined Mom.

"Sammer called me too," Mason said. "I thought I'd bring over some fresh, homemade pound cake to express my sympathies. It's a mighty hard thing, losin' yer pets."

"Thank you, Mason," Mom said, accepting a covered tin. She was tearing up again.

"Now, now, honey, don't start cryin'," Sabrina said, patting Mom on the shoulder. "Maggie is now free of pain, riding around heaven with a diamond saddle on."

"I've never lost a horse, but I lost my favorite dog a few years ago," Mason added. "I *still* think about her."

"Thank you so much for dropping by. Both of you," Mom said. "It means so much."

"Well, we will let you be with your family now. Don't want to overstay our visit. It looks like a storm is brewin' too, so I better be gettin' home. I don't wanna be stuck in a rainstorm in my golf cart," Sabrina said.

"See ya later, Emily," Mason said. "Hang in there, Jules."

"Bye, Sabrina. Bye, Mason." Mom waved.

I was in awe of the sense of community I had just experienced. *My neighbors in New York didn't bring over homemade pound cake on sad occasions . . . and they were ten steps away from my door, not ten miles.*

Turning back into the barn, I walked over to Maggie's stall. It was so empty now. I leaned against the stall door, looking into the pasture. From where I stood, I could see the mound of turned-up soil at the end of her pasture, where she used to stand all day long. Rocky used to stand at the end of his pasture too—both of them together, no matter what time of day, separated only by a pipe-and-cable fence. My mind flooded with images of Rocky and Maggie running around their pastures, galloping in circles or racing each other to the barn. Maggie had always won.

Rocky was making his way to the end of his pasture, taking his post where he would have stood with Maggie all afternoon. Now he stood there alone.

Suddenly, thunder boomed, shaking the entire barn. I flew away from the stall door, backing into Mom, who had been standing quietly behind me. There was a moment of silence, and then it began to pour. I had never seen such a storm.

"Wow," I breathed. "I can't believe it's actually raining."

The torrential downpour veiled everything around me; the rain pounded loudly onto the metal roof of the barn, drowning out every other sound. Mimi and Grandpa joined Mom and me at Maggie's stall. Together, we all stared out at the beautiful rain.

"When it rains, it pours," Grandpa said.

"When it rains, it ruins my hair," Mimi added.

"Never curse the rain, Lorraine," Grandpa retorted.

As Mimi and Grandpa continued their conversation on the woes and wonders of weather, I looked out through the haze of water droplets and thought I saw movement at the end of Maggie's pasture. *Wishful thinking.*

"Jules, look," Mom said, taking my hand as she pointed toward the pasture. Indeed, I had seen movement. The longhorns were filing into Maggie's pasture. Revolution was in the lead, followed by Valentino and then Labor Daisy. The Prides were next, then Clover and P.S., then Tiger Bud. All twenty-seven longhorns proceeded in one by one without a single moo, like silent, reverent giants. As they approached Maggie's grave, they bent their heads to the ground and paused, their noses sniffing the dirt, as if paying homage to her memory. We all watched, speechless, hardly daring to breathe. Soon the whole herd filled the pasture, facing the barn in silence. Revolution then bent her nose to the ground once more, sniffed several times, and mooed a long, extended moo. Rain rolled off her horns and face.

Suddenly, little Tex popped his head through Maggie's stall door. After looking around for a moment, he stepped into the stall and lay down in the exact place where Maggie had breathed her last breath. His mother was nowhere to be seen; he just lay there, seeming to fear nothing, completely at peace.

"Look at Tex, Mom," I said, as if she wasn't staring at him already.

"Tex?" Grandpa asked.

"This is the longhorn we named after you, Dad."

Grandpa looked down at the baby longhorn. "Hi, Tex," he said. Tex looked up at Grandpa intently.

A lightning bolt cracked across the sky. I expected little Tex to run out of the barn, looking for his mother. But he didn't. He stayed absolutely still.

"Isn't he a brave little thing," Grandpa said. I looked up at Grandpa as he wrapped his arm around my shoulder, my hand still in Mom's tight grasp. Tex continued to sit there, sporadically flicking his tail to shoo away the flies.

Then, as quickly as it had begun, the rain stopped. In place of the walls of rain, shafts of sunlight beamed across the pasture and into the barn.

"Oh, there's a break in the rain!" Mimi exclaimed. "Let's quickly get into the car and drive up to the house. We could have gotten electrocuted by all that lightning."

"No we wouldn't have, Lorraine," Grandpa sighed, but Mimi was already trotting off to her car. He looked down at me, rolling his eyes, before reluctantly following Mimi to the car. I turned toward Mom, wondering if we really had to leave. For some reason, the idea of leaving the barn filled me with angst, as if leaving would cause me to lose forever the last fragments of Maggie I still held on to so tightly. Or maybe it was the thought of having to come back to the barn and finding her stall empty.

"It's okay, Jules," Mom said, as if reading my mind. "Let's go get something to eat."

She began walking to the car, but I lingered for a moment as a singular shaft of sunlight suddenly illuminated Maggie's stall, beaming right onto Tex. He blinked as the light filled his dark, dewy eyes, making them sparkle. I couldn't help but feel that the shaft of light meant something, that Tex meant something. *Maybe this is Maggie's way of telling me she is now safe in heaven.* Upon feeling the warmth of the sunlight on his body, Tex laid his head down, completely serene. He really was a brave little longhorn.

If little Tex can be brave, I thought, *I can be brave too.*

Epilogue

essie, come back here!" I yelled. "General . . . No, don't go into the forest, please."

I scrambled around the gravel road, trying to herd my four dogs down to the barn. As independently minded as they were, they all decided to take their own path. General desperately wanted to walk through the forest and chase a few squirrels along the way; Jessie wanted to run through the horse pastures to find some coyotes to bully; Chubbs wanted to find the path with the maximum amount of shade; and dear old Buster walked submissively at my heels with his husky panting.

Before General could disappear into the forest forever, I grabbed on to his collar. Conveniently for him, his collar slipped right from his neck as he flopped onto the ground, refusing to move. "General!" I muttered, shoving the collar back onto his neck. *I guess I'm going to have to tighten that later.*

Meanwhile, I heard Jessie force her way through the pipe-and-cable fence into the horse pastures. "Jessie, stop right there!" I abandoned my attempts to lift General to a standing position and ran across the road to Jessie. Reaching through the fence, I pulled her back under the fence and onto the road. She looked quite perturbed that I had thwarted her plans of gallivanting around the ranch. Making my way back to General, who still had not rejoined my caravan, I snatched Chubbs, who had decided to start eating grass.

"Chubbs, you know grass makes you sick. And who do you think is going to clean up the house after you decide to throw up phlegm-covered grass?"

After finally getting General and Chubbs back to the road, I found Buster rolling around, trying to scratch his back. When he stood up, his long black hair was coated with a nice dusting of dirt, grass, and sticker burs. "Really, Buster? Who's going to brush you off now?"

"Jules, are you coming?" Mom asked. She was walking ahead and was almost to the barn.

"I'm coming! I'm just also trying to make sure the dogs come too."

"General, Buster, Jessie, Chubbs, come on, you guys," Mom yelled. At the sound of Mom's voice, all four dogs ran toward her, obediently answering her call.

I see where their loyalty lies. What am I, chopped liver?

Nevertheless, I quickly followed the dogs up the hill and into the barn.

"Good morning, Rocky! Good morning, R2!" I called. It was still strange not hearing Maggie's nicker welcome me. I purposefully avoided looking at her old stall as I made my way through the barn. While Mom walked into the feed room, I walked to the hay stall and began scaling the bales of hay. Now quite adept at hay bale climbing, I reached the top in no time and began pulling apart the flakes of hay, throwing them to the floor. Out of habit, I grabbed a third flake before realizing my mistake. My stomach turned over, making me feel slightly nauseous. Maggie seemed so far away, gone forever.

R2 whinnied from her stall, knocking me from my thoughts.

"Hold on a minute, I'm coming!" I said. Gathering all the hay into my arms, I walked into R2's stall and delivered her breakfast. "There you go, you silly pony," I said, patting her on the neck. She pinned her ears, wanting to be left alone to eat. "All right, all right . . ."

Several weeks had passed since Maggie's death and I had learned that life does not pause while you learn to deal with grief. Instead, the world keeps on turning, keeping you on your feet. The ranch still needed attention, horses still needed feeding, cows still needed finding, and school still needed attending. Not a moment passed during the day that I did not think about Maggie, and sometimes I wondered if my life would ever regain normalcy. Maggie's absence was a large abyss I had yet to fully understand. *How could something I loved so much be gone from my life forever?* It was as if a gaping hole had suddenly been cut in the fabric of my life. Yet I found that life was made up of moments, and if I could just make it through that one moment, I could face the next.

"There, Rocky boy," I said, flinging his hay into his feed trough. He was already eating his Equine Senior, barely registering my presence. I leaned over and wrapped my arms around his neck. Some of my anxieties melted away, my whole body relaxing. "You're such a good boy," I said. Rocky looked up at me. I could still see the traces of loneliness in his eyes. He, too, was learning to deal with life without Maggie.

"Jules," Mom started, "I'm going to sweep the barn. How about you get the stalls?"

"Sure thing," I answered. Exiting Rocky's stall, I started walking to the back of the barn to retrieve the wheelbarrow and pitchfork. Instead of finding a wheelbarrow and pitchfork, however, I was greeted by something else entirely.

"Mom!" I exclaimed.

"What is it?" Mom ran through the barn and arrived at my side. "Oh no, we cannot keep another dog."

Right beside the wheelbarrow sat a brown lab, happily snapping at the flies that circled around her head. Her coat was a soft, chocolate brown with lighter brown markings on her hind legs, giving her the appearance that she had been splattered with mud. Obviously, she was a lab-slash-mutt. Upon seeing me, the lab hopped up, barking several times in greeting. I could swear she was smiling.

"Where did she come from?" I asked.

"I have no idea."

Before Mom and I could do anything, the dog walked past us and into the barn, enthusiastically greeting all the other dogs. Thankfully, they got along just fine. Jessie did seem to assert her authority, standing as tall as she could and aloofly lifting her head as the new dog walked near, clearly imparting that she was still the queen of the roost.

"It doesn't look like she has any dog tags," Mom said.

I shook my head. The lab had an old, tattered purple collar, but no tags were present.

"I'm going to call the corner store to see if anyone has reported a missing dog," Mom said, walking through the barn to get her phone. "Don't touch her, Jules! We don't know if she has rabies or if she's had any vaccinations," Mom added over her shoulder.

"Got it."

The brown lab barked several times as Mom passed, seeming to tell her hello. It was a remarkably friendly bark, almost as if she was trying to engage in conversation. I reentered the barn and watched the dog in wonder. *Do dogs usually show up and join a family just like this?*

Everyone except Jessie trailed the new dog closely, as if interrogating her to find out about her past. She casually ignored them, however, instead hopping up into the old white rocking chair as if she were a human. Staring straight at me, she lifted her head in the air and barked three times, the rocking chair swaying precariously.

"What's your story?" I asked her. She barked twice. "Okay, let's try out some names . . . Daisy? No. Coco? No. Donut? No. Princess? No." I stopped. "I'm not having any luck here, am I?" She barked.

"No one has reported a lost dog," Mom said, walking up beside me.

"Yay! We can keep her!"

"We are not keeping her, Jules."

"Mom, I'm sorry to break it to you, but I don't think she's going anywhere soon."

The dog sat in the rocking chair, looking at the other dogs who swarmed below her, acting as if she ruled the place. Jessie did not look pleased. Mom sighed.

"So, what should we call her?"

"I have no idea."

"How about . . ."

"Queenie," Mom said, finally resigned to the fact that we now had a new addition to our pack of dogs. "We will call her Queenie, because she is taking over the place like a queen." The lab began to bark, wagging her tail rapidly.

"I think she likes her name," I said. I walked over to her and rubbed her ears. She looked at me with wide eyes, her pink tongue falling out the side of her mouth. She barked twice.

"She sure barks a lot," Mom said.

"She's just trying to communicate. Aren't you, Queenie?"

Queenie barked.

"All right, Jules. We need to go check the cows before it gets too hot today. Let's go drop the dogs back off at the house. And we have to figure out what we're going to do with Queenie. I'll need to put a sign up in case someone is looking for her."

"Okay, I'm coming," I said. Mom began leading the way out of the barn—General, Jessie, Buster, and Chubbs following her, anxious to get to the air-conditioning. Queenie, however, stayed seated in her rocking chair. "Come on, Queenie. You don't want to be left behind, do you?" Queenie instantly jumped from the rocking chair, but instead of running to me, she darted to the other end of the barn, stopping right in front of Maggie's stall.

That's weird.

"Queenie, let's go." Queenie didn't move. "Please don't make me walk over there." Queenie barked. Resigning myself to the fact that Queenie would not come on her own accord, I walked over to her. When I arrived at Maggie's stall door, I saw something move in the far corner of the stall. I gasped as my eyes focused on the glimmering image that stood gallantly in the shadows. It was Maggie, except she was draped in brilliant light, her coat now one hundred times more vibrant, as if made from flakes of pure gold. Her eyes were clear, free from pain and free from sadness. Instead, her body radiated an untainted joy I had never felt before.

Maggie?

Her eyes looked straight into mine. The anxieties and sorrow I had battled for the past weeks seemed to melt from my bones, replaced with an understanding that everything was okay—that Maggie was okay.

"Don't worry, Jules," Maggie seemed to say. "I am okay. I am free from pain. I am happy. I am at peace. You be happy too."

Tears filled my eyes. As I blinked to clear the tears, the image of Maggie began to blur until it fully disappeared. I stood in complete silence for a moment, not wanting to move. Looking down at Queenie, I saw that she was still staring at the stall. Then she looked at me, barked, and starting walking from the barn.

"Jules, are you okay?" Mom yelled from the road.

"Yeah," I answered. My ears suddenly became attuned to the loud hum of the cicadas that filled the air and the melodious tunes of the many birds that filled the trees. As the slight breeze brushed against my face, I could smell a trace of Maggie's beautiful scent in the air. I ran out of the barn, my heart pounding in my chest, my feet feeling lighter with every step, and emerged into the sunlight. *"You be happy too"* resonated in my mind.

I will, Maggie. I will.